I0533916

OPERATION HOPSCOTCH

Hardley The
Child's Game

M A LONGENECKER

Copyright © 2011 M A Longenecker
All rights reserved.

ISBN: 0615431488
ISBN-13: 9780615431482

Dedication

To my Daughter, Ruth whose love and encouragement sparked my creativity and made this journey possible. To my son, Harold and his wife, Merle who are always available whenever the computer crashes; And, my neighbors: Rich, who supplied daily doses of e-mail humor and encouragement, and John, who would like to see Missy reappear in Book II.

Chapters

1. Prologue

Titan Dump, Abandoned WWII Bunker
San Pedro, California

The tallest of the four, masked men yelled, "Sit down and shut up! The first to move gets a surprise! And, that means you, Mr. Grand, What-ever-the-hell!"

"I'm sorry I can't oblige you at this moment, you see you have chosen a very poor time to interrupt this peaceful gathering. I'm quite certain your day would improve if you could see your way clear to joi..." The report of a handgun caused the beloved Grand Supervisor to slump to the floor in a fetal position.

"I don't think so!" The man's eyes glistened with the thrill of success. When he was sure he had everyone's attention, he started to make his way down the back row stopping in front of the first man. "Put your cash and your jewelry into this bag – NOW!"

The man complied, placing a single dollar bill into the bag.

"So, you are the SMART GUY in this room, huh? Well, try this on for size!" He hit the man across the side of his head with the butt of his gun. When the injured man remained standing, the tall man hit him again! "So, Mr. Smart Guy, you finally got my message! Gemme your jewelry – NOW!"

Not waiting for the fallen Brother to attempt an answer, the next seated Cabal Member said, "We don't wear jewelry! We bow to no graven image; No idols! Our Lord forbids it!" The speaker had a smile on his lips as he crumpled to the floor in response to a bullet.

At that moment the remaining assembly stood and began singing…to the top of their collective voices, "Give praise to Jehovah, His Kingdom Devine, the light that is shin…" Every voice stopped when the first hundred rounds sprayed across the standing men. One of the three remaining men in black, at the front of the room, was laughing as the clip of his Oozy fell empty to the floor. "You take over, Sup. After all, this is really your party, not ours." The FBI Supervisor rose to his feet, "I paid you well. You missed a few back here."

A momentary hush fell over the room. The few remaining began to sing until the last voice was stilled.

It would be a while before the mystery of the Titan Dump Massacre would be solved.

∽

2. Los Angeles

The Miracle Mile was longer than any mile, WWII vet, Braden Jacques Cartwright ("Jac" pronounced "Jack" by his friends), had ever walked. Five plus miles! He had no way of knowing his information neglected to include the fact that while the Miracle Mile *was* on Wilshire Boulevard, it did not begin until Fairfax Boulevard, according to the locals. And, some, five miles away! He didn't mind too much. It was a beautiful, spring day and, the potential out-come of his labors made every step worth the effort! His last four hours of job hunting had reinforced his belief that there was, *a damn good* chance of get-ting the job he wanted! He would check them all… law firms, insurance companies, and commercial offices! So far, everyone he contacted had been very friendly and interested. Many acted as though they had expected him to arrive. Jac chalked it up to his resume. He reasoned it was *pretty good*! He was First in his law class, outstanding in the Navy, with commendations, and no brushes with the Law. *And, a pretty fair pilot.* While the interviewers didn't have a place for him in the moment, they told him to

1

keep in touch, and suggested he continue his search without stopping until he had contacted every potential company, especially, insurance companies. *Jac wondered at the time how it was that everyone he spoke with gave the same advice. And, how did they know his primary objective was to get a position in an Insurance office? Was Los Angeles experiencing a dearth of legal professionals?*

Jac hoped his yellow pad of new contacts would prove invaluable in time to come. A man long on goals! Short on experience; with an unstoppable drive! By his calculations, he expected his efforts to provide most of the comforts he desired. All within nine or ten, *short* months! He had refused to listen when dorm buddies had said he was crazy. He had never been afraid of hard work. He ordained, "January, 1950 to be *THE* month for celebrating his first hundred-thousand dollar verdict!" *Not necessarily, a viable consideration in 1949.* For just the moment, Jacques Brandon Cartwright felt invincible!

Networking; Doc said networking was more important than any other activity Jac could possibly do to insure the level of success he wanted! "Don't let a single opportunity pass you by without jotting down everything about the contact. Things that might seem unimportant at the time could become the difference between making an acquaintance and finding a wealthy client." *Little did Jac know contacts would provide him more than he ever dreamed possible! More importantly, very soon, they would save his professional life from disaster!* In no way did he know what lay ahead!

Jac smiled as he thought of home, and the events that eventually lead him to Los Angeles.

It was a perfect spring morning in Warsaw, Illinois that greeted him as he quietly closed the front door, his rope-secured suitcase and gym bag in hand. The Navy had accepted him for flight-training! He only had to walk twenty paces or so to the train track. His dog, Shep, his oldest, and more accurately, his only friend, followed at his heel. It wasn't until he was seated on the moving train that he realized two disturbing thoughts. One, only the dog had said goodbye, not any member of his family. And, two he felt absolutely no discomfort leaving his home and family. He was, after all, going (ostensibly, as far as the Folks knew) to war!

Truth be known, the Navy was his way out! He was sure the President would declare war on Germany very soon. He was determined 'fly' not 'walk' when it happened! It would be an embarrassment to allow anyone to know the depth and direction of his feelings. Most were jumbled within a network of fear and uncertainty.

It was a strange feeling of excitement or thrill; he didn't know which! He didn't know how to classify the feelings since they had never been experienced before! Just the thought of possible success affected him in a dozen different ways! Jac knew only one thing for certain: This was his escape! And, he would never look back! Perhaps a visit to see, mom, nothing more.

The train ride passed quickly. And then…there IT was! Navy Pier! Chicago, sun bleached and radiant, came into sight. Jac's plan was beginning! Ninety days of training would give him a Commission in the Navy. Law school after if he came home safely.

He would ultimately became a squadron-leader off a flat-top, the USS CARD. Shy as he was, he enjoyed being in-charge. And did a damn good job of it, earning him several commendations. He completed his four years of Military Service, and returned home before going to Washburn School of Law, in Topeka, Kansas.

With the War over, he had every reason to believe *life would be different at home.* Sadly, the only difference was four more years of peeling-paint from the section house where he lived, and every male friend, lucky enough to return home, was *four years older*! His ship-board "doc," and mentor, Doc Harks, a misplaced pediatrician, took every opportunity to mentor Jac in the ways of city life. Doc reasoned they got along so well, because both were out of place. Jac remembered Doc's last words, "Use your GI Bill and get yourself an education." He had asked, "Where are your dog tags?" When Jac answered, "In my duffle." Doc pressed Jac's hand with what looked like a mosaic cross on a chain and said, "Always remember; life's like a game of Hopscotch, one bad move and you have to start over unless you use you lagger well!" Jac remember thinking that at the time, he had never played a game of hopscotch; after all, it was a girl's game, and he had no idea whatsoever, what a lagger was used for! Oh, well, *he knew Doc meant well.*

3. In Another Part of Town

Seven miles from the Miracle Mile, telephones began to ring in a room behind what ostensibly was a shoe-shine stand. Three elevated seats and a lone operator. No customers. Beyond a well-insulated door, an un-seen, back room held excited voices affirming the Grand Supervisor's recommendations for replacing an ailing, beloved, Grand Supervisor.

"First, we must come to grips with what has happened to our murdered Brethren. Because our Blessed Lord has promised Salvation and life everlasting we should celebrate the journey of our Brothers in Him as they take their place at his right hand. We can do this by continuing our search for the Chosen One. There is NO time for mourning the physically dead." *The Supervisor even impressed* himself! *Such composure! Admirable, when you consider he had the missing Concordia of The Devine! No, he wasn't ready to share the information; but he was ready to enlist assistance in sorting information that would to lead HIM to the location of some 'much sought after gold.' Finding the Concordia brought him a great sense of accomplishment, satisfaction, and invincibility!*

The supervisor continued, "Second, let us forge ahead with renewed allegiance to our quest; the recruiting of a very, special, young Vet, who is possibly the long-awaited Chosen One!" *The Chosen One would lead every member of the Cabal to life everlasting!*

Within minutes, phones shared the news with all the Western Cabals. "We believe the Chosen has been found," was the message! After all, the young man appeared to meet every requirement as the holder of the key to their beloved, Concordia of The Devine in the section of Promises. "*A child will come from the lowest of the longest river. He shall be faire of hair, strong of limb, and possess the heart of the lion. He will have the mark of the Holy One on each breast which beneath each, shall dwell the keys to the Code of Devine Concordia.*" Only the Supervisor knew the Concordia had already been found. His persistence in continuing the quest of a book he already had in his possession was for more than just *a book! Much more!*

None of the assembled understood how the keys would work. Theirs was but a singular objective; to be recognized as the ones to whom the reward was to be given. After all, according to the learned Supervisor they were the group God had selected to be alive at such a momentous occasion. The sense of *prominence* in the Lord's Plan was adequate for the Believers! Theirs was not a quest for personal gain, rather, the promise of *life everlasting! Not so with the Supervisor, He was too smart to pass up a such a perfect* *opportunity to reap the 'real' reward. "Who needs God?"*He had to catch himself; He had almost spoken aloud! *"That would have been GREAT!"*

Who could have predicted the Supervisor's miracle of *'chance?'* He knew the members of the Cabal believed the Concordia actually existed. His finding it *was* a major coup!

"Cabal members are so stupid! Not a brain in a carload of them! The poor Dopes! The information was right in front of their collective noses! And, they thought I was the crazy one when I insisted on reading all the old papers found in the inherited, Illinois Cabal building. Rat droppings and all!"

Being able to quote from the Concordia made the Supervisor sound more like the "Chosen" than just a *faithful Brother.* Having the Concordia gave him huge advantage in assembling a small cadre of highly qualified Brethren (who came from all walks of life) to assist with the necessary exploration (ferreting) of all available history found in the old files. Unlike the Supervisor, they didn't know what they were looking for; they thought they were helping to develop Cabal history.

"When they finish, and if they've done a thorough job, all I'll have to do is collate the golden spike information left by the International Bible Students. They must have been saps of a first water! I can't imagine people deliberately turning their backs on a fortune in gold! That God and Mammon crap is not to be believed! It's beyond me!"

The Cabal's parent group had been scrupulous in keeping Elder Elite Records away from the General Membership. While the New group held very little with the old regime, they thought better of destroying any of the hundred and fifty year old files that were left behind. The old quarters, now ravaged by time and neglect, still held a basement full of old missives, colorfully bound books and an assortment of hand-written, religious articles; all mentioning the existence of the Concordia and the possible location of *God's Gift to the Anointed*. The Supervisor had the distinct feeling it was a gift of gold, more than likely, the missing spikes. Thankfully, the old relic was one of the few, older buildings not razed in Warsaw, Illinois.

The Supervisor had rented the room for a month. Warsaw had little to offer in the way of comfortable, temporary quarters. It was however, rich with the history of its patriotic population serving and sup-porting all the Nation's vital war efforts. And, proudly displayed a voluminous, Who's Who of military Per-sonnel in spite of the town's dwindling population. The remaining families of Warsaw proudly remembered their brave veterans with a Memorial next to Albert Mill Museum. The Supervisor thought it uncanny; the papers and books were like new, untouched by neglect and the elements. He didn't take time to wonder how this was accomplished. *Thankfully, it*

only took him six days to find his prize. He managed a broad smile when he thought, "On the seventh day I rested!" All he needed now was the exact location of the twelve golden spikes.

4. The Coup!

The Cabal Brothers had done a splendid job researching! The Supervisor found a strong correlation between Cabal requirements for the Chosen One, and a student named in a scandal at Devon College in Carthage, Illinois…Jac's college. It fit oral Cabal history like a glove! Jac lived in the river-bottoms of the Mississippi; he had reddish-blond hair; he had two scars on his chest; and he was a decorated flying ace in the war! The school came under scrutiny when it was learned the hazing practices of one of the Greek fraternities sanctioned the burning of the letter 'V' on each breast.

What a coup! A single sheet of paper amongst the accumulated mass of research; the headline on the front page of the Warsaw Bulletin proclaimed…"the banishment of a popular campus group because of hazing practices." The article continued to speak to the need of protecting youth, like Braden J. Cartwright, age twenty, popular fraternity member who would be graduating soon with plans to become a Navy flyer." *The Supervisor, more than pleased with himself, was breathless from the excitement of his*

13

"find!" Now, all he had to do was 'get in good with the kid's family and do a little specialized containment.' Especially, with the father! A little flattery and a couple of bucks could probably go a long way in getting the Hick to help him out! Something the Supervisor knew all too well, how to do! No problem! He had friends in high places! He removed a small notebook from a breast pocket. Let's see, "First I need to make some contacts for local info on the family. How many kids? Is there a mother? Thank God for my friend, the Navy Doc, he said he thought the kid fit the description of the Chosen One to a tea! Poor sucker, devout believer, always wanting to do 'nice' for all the young sailors! What a Sap!

Now that the kid's in LA, I'll get JM to get next to him, she's a great Agent! She can get any man to do anything she wants! Okay, let's see; special note to self, "Contact all Cabal members working in the Wilshire Corridor; contact General Membership to stay alert for a special message from me!" The Supervisor closed his notebook and was about to put it away when a thought hit him! "My GOD! I almost forgot about White House Insurance! I'll bet I can kill two birds with one stone if I'm lucky! I'll give it a try!" That smug smile crossed Supervisor's face once again.

∾

5. Finding A Job

Jac checked the last name and address on the legal pad; White House Insurance, "Located On The Miracle Mile At Carthay Circle Drive." *Jac had cut the entire ad from the paper because the specific reference to the location intrigued him. He could only reason 'there must be something very special about this location.' Going up the stairs, flanked by four Doric Columns, Jac thought, 'this is IT!' He had a sense he would get exactly what he asked for in terms of an office, law books, a telephone, and a part-time secretary (to start his private practice). Of course, giving 'them' a half-day of his time…in exchange!*

The huge doors opened into a spacious reception room, flanked on all sides by imposing portraits of the company founder, sundry large oils, a single hand-carved mahogany desk and chair, a pleasant, middle-aged receptionist, and little else. A fair assessment of the room would be everything 'museum quality;' at the very least. Very impressive! Stairs to the executive offices gave-up a squeak with every encounter of his size 13 shoe. The sparkling exterior and downstairs reception area belied the rather shabby interior of the second floor. Jac wondered what the building was used for before it became the Whitehouse? The furniture had seen better days, probably in-place since the early thirties, lots of opaque glass-cubes serving as room dividers, ratty shades at the large windows, no one speaking, everyone yelling, and an over-powering odor of cigars; lots of cigars! If there was one thing Jac hated, it was the smell of cigars!

Something his dad did every day of every week! Smoke! Jac and his mother would go into coughing spasms that deprived them of breath. Dad's response was to threaten leaving them alone, no water, no heat, and no food, 'if they didn't shut-up; now!' The smoking tirade was one of many tirades, well rehearsed over Jac's entire life living at home.

Life on the Mississippi could have been great, were it not for the presence of a very angry father and a mother divested of self-esteem. Jac's diagnosis, lack of Gumption! When his mother couldn't tolerate what was happening, she would disappear to her special place on the river bank, soak her feet, and repeat the Rosary. As far as Jac could tell, it never seemed to do more than aggravate his dad. Which, in turn, dad took out on his sister; 'a chip off mother's block,' according to dad. Passive to a point of igniting one of Jack's major frustrations, his sister swallowed insults' and denied any emotional or physical abuse...regardless of the abuser!

An example was the recurring drama played out by a local family of bullies. They called his sister... Jap Nose, not that her nose was bigger or looked like she was Japanese. It was just their stupid excuse to treat her as the 'enemy.' Meaning, 'enemies get tied to any available tree.' Or, worse! Throw mud on a Sunday dress. Jac reasoned the behavior might be in response to the fact that no one in the family had been seen as 'fit' for military service. It was assumed, by all the town folks, the family was a pickle short of a picnic and took license to do whatever they wanted! Jac could never understand convoluted thinking; "why in the world did they keep voting for a sheriff that reasoned, 'boys will be boys?'" To make matters worse, mother would calmly ask, "Jac, would you please find your sister, and, and untie her." Sure, his mother sounded a little wacky! But, no one had better say anything against her. The whole town knew that would insure the wrath of Jac! There were times Jac wanted to scream! He tried to remember; hadn't he once heard that Irish women were strong both physically and emotionally. He wondered what could have happened. His mother exhibited, little or none of either attribute.

Jac's *reverie* was broken when a not-too-imposing, middle-aged, pear-shaped man introduced himself as Emmery Gant, office manager, and asked if could direct Jac to Sales. Introducing himself as an attorney, Jac, was immediately ushered to one of the cubicles where he was given a seven-page application. He politely refused a cold drink, but accepted the manager's (somewhat monotone) suggestions about some of the questions and how they might be enhanced to catch the Boss's eye. "The Boss hate 'kids' and thinks the war has wasted all the good men and only left 'snot-nosed kids!' Jac was admonished to use the backside of the papers to talk about the grown-up stuff he had accomplished. Like, all the War experiences, blood and guts; good stuff, he eats that up, if you know what I mean!"

Jac, complied. Everything was completed as suggested (*instructed*). He had more than enough questions building in his mind about the lack of professional ethics being displayed. The pervasive feeling of 'who gives a damn' made him feel most uncomfortable. *He had been told by his professors that he could expect to be treated with quiet dignity and respect... as an Attorney.* He didn't expect the 'budding-up' he had just experienced with Mr. Gant. He had absolutely no plans to become some stranger's best buddy or pal. He had always been told 'at arm's length away' was the best distance to maintain between himself and anyone else. *He wondered what the manager had in store for the relationship, should he happen to be hired.*

Very little time was lost in kiss-up, Jac remembering his military training, came directly to what he wanted, and what he was willing to give in exchange. To his surprise, his offer was accepted on the spot! Mr. Gant apparently had more control than Jac gave him credit for, considering his general appearance and his lack-luster demeanor. Jac's office would be to the rear of the executive offices. So far, so good.

The arrangement, was to provide everything Jac asked for, including an over-sexed, thirty-something, 'Missy' secretary, with a great rack and bad breath, Missy expressed her delight to be working with "**you**, Mr. Cartwright!" *Missy was glad Jac couldn't read her mind, 'A tall, young, good-looking guy with big hands, and you know what they say about that,* "How do you like your coffee, Honey?"

"Missy, just call me Jac, spelled j-a-c, pronounced like j-a-c-k. Black is fine."

"God, talk about PICKY!" *Under her breath,* "Wait 'til Brooksie hears about this!"

6. The Next Elder Meeting

The Elite Cabal Elders were never to hear of the newspaper that told of the Collage hazing scandal. The Supervisor would allow everyone to believe the Lord had Blessed him with Devine guidance. He would not allow himself to relax until he had the gold in-hand. He had to plan his next moves very carefully. He would be manipulating a more educated people this time.

The Elders had reviewed the information provided by the Supervisor. The ferreted information, on the One Who Bore the Scars, was well received by everyone! The young man's character, and demeanor were favorable; "easy-going temperament, with a deep love and respect for human life. A handsome man of tall-stature, intelligent, well-developed body, and charismatic smile! Most important, 'A beguiling naiveté.'" *Cabal members, like sheep, believed Devine guidance had indeed lead the Supervisor to identify Braden Jacques Cartwright as the only, true Chosen One.*

The Supervisor's plan was to entice Jac into the scenario by inventing a legal problem centered in Warsaw…Jac's birthplace. Only he, Supervisor to all, Cabal member by night and valued, government worker by day, knew or thought he knew, the *touted* location of more gold than even he could have imagined! Better yet, the gold was thought to be in an Illinois hotel. The Supervisor was certain it was the old Warsaw Depot Hotel…Jac's birth-home! The most important information came when his research coincidentally told of an early crime where, "… golden spikes had been stolen from a museum and were believed to be hidden in an old hotel in Warsaw, Illinois." *It can only be imagined what this information did for the Supervisor.* The Supervisor screamed (with-in himself), *"Not just the Concordia! I will have the fortune in GOLD!"*

The Supervisor was too focused to carelessly miss this life-sized opportunity to "make-it!' He didn't wait to establish-as-fact the Warsaw Hotel as the actual depository of the spikes. HE was on a roll! Get a ticket, fly to Illinois and get the prima-fascia. In his mind, there was too much evidence! Jac's family would be the Supervisor's first order of business. He had friends in high places who would could provide, (should they become necessary), mind-altering drugs…for a price. His plan was to skillfully develop a situation where his "day job" could provide the necessary players for the drama that had to be played-out at night. He was sure the mother and daughter would been a cinch! Mr. Cartwright, known as a previous owner, might be a different matter! He had only met him once; the time he decided to check on the authenticity of the Warsaw newspaper. The Supervisor had never met a more cantankerous individual. Brash, rude, loud, indifferent to others, egotistical, superior in imagined intelligence, and more; cruel to his family. The Supervisor had to admit that if questioned, he would have to admit he felt a bit sorry for the Vet. The only problem being faced at the moment was the Vet's father who insisted that "No one would be allowed to enter the Hotel without his 'Blessing' (translated, "Pay me!"). Oh well, No Problem! He knew his original plan, to butter the old fool up with smart talk and a few bucks, would work! If not, there was always the use of drugs. No matter! No Hick was going to take advantage of his 'treasure!' He needed to return to California as soon as possible!

The Brethren were right where *he* wanted them! The Elite Cabal Elders Hanging on every word he spoke! The only 'fly in the ointment' was the ailing Grand Supervisor, who thought little of anyone who would deign to boast of manipulating in any way, the Lord's word!

Everything was working perfectly for the Cabal Supervisor, and would continue to do so. Nothing was going to interfere with his 'promotion!' When the time came, it would be easy enough to excise the discs that were said to be under the twin scars on the Vet's chest. He couldn't help but feel proud in the knowledge he and he alone held the 'Key to every-one's eternity.' Elevation to the next Cabal station would suffice until his quest was finally recognized, and the World standing at attention before him! And, HE, the one elected by Devine power…would RULE! The Supervisor fingered the aging, cross-like lagger hanging under his shirt. Its representation and full meaning brought a great sense of accomplishment, satisfaction and invincibility! All this would become possible because he, and he alone, had found the Concordia! *Generations before him who searched for the concordance…BE DAMNED! Memory, like avarice, in his case, ignored the wealth of information gleaned from his ancestors; he wanted the Quest to be known as his own. Forsaking honor and respect, he had seized every opportunity to steal credit leading to the location of the concordance.* He had to smile! As a second, ego-boosting irony; the Supervisor kept the twelfth-century document in plain sight of the Brethren. Safe, dry, in a teakwood chest beneath the Cabal dais…which had no physical key! *The Supervisor was so full of himself at the moment, he failed to consider, 'who before him knew to place the "key to the Concordia" under the hazing-scars? And, what was the relationship to the Cabal?*

Self aggrandizement was such an exhilarat-ing feeling he had to excuse himself from the Cabal Elders. A secret door that opened to the alley allowed for a quick retreat. He had to think things out. The fresh air quickened the Supervisor's musings. Smil-ing to himself, he continued visualizing his advancement to Superior Supervisor, only one step away from Grand Supervisor of the Cabal which would no doubt be forth coming at the next Western Assembly…a month away. His mind began to race! There were still a few ends to take care of before he could claim his assignment finished. There were to be NO foul-ups! *He chose a secluded bench in the nearby park. Secrecy, no matter when or where, was always paramount with the Supervisor!*

He opened a small detective's notebook, fat with notations covering his research. The notations were numeric and alphabetic symbols, only the Supervisor knew how to decipher the more important part of the Vet's voluminous file!

7. The Cohort

In a small, cramped, closet of a room, in a nether-reach of the Depot Hotel, sat a pot-bellied man of some sixty-years, or so. Pencil between the teeth, and a green, dealers cap on his balding head. His cigar had long gone out, but the man appeared not to notice. A broad smile nearly caused the pencil to fall to the floor. The man spoke out loud, *"Damn It! I hate when that happens!"* Adjusting the pencil, he turned to the next page on a small notebook, *"Well, do tell! We got us a second Sucker! "Just call me The Supervisor, he says!" Ain't that a crock! They travel a couple of thousand miles and think they own the town! Well, Buster, I am thinking I've got you cold! So, Mr. Goody Two Shoes, how did you like my writing, pretty good, huh? Talk about a Dumb Cluck; your eyes almost went buggy, or was it your pants when I said I saved out some of the papers you were so interested in; poor Babe, I can only imagine why! Yah, I thought it was a pretty good touch to put in a little about the Kid."* The old man adjusted his rickety chair, and relit his cigar. *"The old lady would kill me if she saw me smoking. Sometimes I think the only reason I smoke is to remind her that I ALWAYS know where her goat is tied."* With the movement of a skilled surgeon, the man lofted the page with wet ink and blew away any particles from the well- aged appearing paper.

The work was an almost perfect, machine-like script. Not surprising that his writing was quite remark-able; he had been taught by the same penmanship teacher who taught his mother and grandmother. "I know that City Slicker is going to come back. When I mentioned I had a kid that had a rotten experience in school, I really had him going!" A furled brow gave him pause, *"How in the hell am I going to talk my kid into going along with the plan?"*

8. The Job

Jac caught a trolley back to the Y. He was so excited about the outcome of this day, he decided to celebrate! He knew the YMCA did not allow any alcohol, so he planned to visit the small bar on the corner. He really didn't drink. He didn't care too much for the taste. The smell was worse. But, he did want to celebrate! He figured he would have a drink with his meal, and hope someone, other than the barkeep, might talk to him so he could share his great, good fortune. *Jac had a way of planning everything to a gnat's eyebrow, leaving little room for the unexpected.* Some might reason it was a healthy way to behave considering he was in an unfamiliar environment.

The Tick Tock sounded empty. Black as a hole at first. So much for the thought about having any company. Well, there was still the *'bartender'* (he was trying to use urban vernacular). She turned-out to be a very intelligent, college girl, named Janice, who was happy to have a customer to talk to. She regaled Jac with information about the many points-of-special interest in and round Los Angeles. She touted local music and stage as being recognized as some of the best in the country. Jac had many questions about the stage productions, having been introduced to *culture* in the Navy. He had seen Twelfth Night and Two Gentlemen from Verona. He wasn't too interested in orchestras or operas.

While Janice volunteered volumes of information, Jac was lost in the memory of the time he had embarrassed himself at a Navy Hail and Farewell in the Officer's Club. He blew his nose in a buffet napkin. *Most of the other JGs were from wealthy families of the Atlantic Seaboard variety. Ritzy homes, ritzy clothes, and ritzy schools. Nothing like the two-story, slat-board Section house for railroad workers he grew up in. Sparsely furnished rooms, one bath on each floor, no running water. Water had to be carried by hand and poured into a common bowl or tub. Jac's mother did most of wash, with Jac, who hung clothes on a line and would take them down and fold. Grandma, Diffy, did all the cooking. Simple Irish fare. Fresh breads, some meat, and heavy on gravy. Jac had to laugh at himself when he remembered how he told a Navy cook that his pie was not 'chewy enough;' It was too flaky! He didn't know any better. That's the way granny always made pie! Little wonder the cook never served him pie as long as he was on that Ship! There were so many things he needed to learn. The Navy had enough time to make a passable gentleman out of him. His father screamed at Jac on his first visit home, "The God-Damn Navy needs to fight wars, not make sissies! Hold your fork like a man, you look like a God damn pansy!"*

One good thing. The visit home before leaving for the war made his mother very happy! She had only one favor to ask of Jac. Save Uncle Joe… from himself! The poor man lived with mom's sisters who were very religious. No alcohol! Always on Joe's back about going to Hell, and that drinking was leading him to perdition in a hand basket! No wonder the poor man drank. He probably could have gotten by okay if he didn't, so generously, exhibit some of the behaviors he was wont to do.

Like leading their cow across the trestle which spanned the Mississippi from Iowa to Illinois. He wanted to sell the cow for 'wine money.' Or, the time the sheriff put a ball and chain on his leg, because he was very adept at escape, only to find Joe had picked up the ball and escaped, once again. And, to the Sheriff's embarrassment sent the ball back C.O.D.. Good old Uncle, Joe.

There was the other time he was taken onto court by a neighbor because he was playing the piano and singing so loudly the neighbor on the next acre couldn't sleep, "Your honor, several nights running, caterwauling and loud piano playing, it's more than a person should have to endure!"

Joe asked the court to let him act as his own attorney. On cross-examining, Joe asked the complainant, "If I were playing so loudly please tell the court what I was playing! The poor woman was at a loss, she said she didn't know. "You see Judge, I was playing so softly, she couldn't name it! The Judge dismissed all charges. Suffice it to know, Joe never knew how to play a note. Just bang on the keys. As for singing, just like his nephew, Joe had always been told to move his lips and not sing, a real embarrassment to Jac when he attended Devon College. You would think a Christian school might have had enough compassion to allow Jac to sing, not just move his mouth like uncle Joe.

Then there was the time Joe took the local newspaper to court. The offence…the paper made a misprint when they said Joe Walters had been in jail thirty times in thirty days, and should have read, 'Joe Walters has been in jail thirty times in a year.' Joe won, again. He won for 'pain and suffering,' he won just enough to get s drunk again. In spite of all the evidence to the contrary, mother was sure that if Jac would only visit wearing his white uniform, Uncle, Joe would be so embarrassed he would stop drinking!

Jac remembered feeling very embarrassed as he entered the County jail. Joe was really happy to see him! He invited him into his cell; You would need to know that Joe was in jail so often his cell had more of his personal belongings than his room at home. Joe, made Jac comfortable and offered him a drink! He always had a drink 'sequestered,' only for unexpected visitors, of course. Needless to say, mom was really unhappy. One, because the visit didn't change anything, and two, because Jac took the drink! So much for visits home. It would be quite some time before the next visit. It was a promise Jac made to himself, one he intended to keep!

By now, Janice, had just about run out of up-coming cultural events. Jac was back! He hadn't heard too much of what she had to say, so he covered by asking her which attraction she would pick if she were able to go out for the night. She shared her love of the theater and said the movie Red Shoes was in town and would probably select Friday, it's only three days away, but I think I can get good tickets.

"Okay, sounds great, Janice! Here's the money, you get the tickets and Friday, I'll pick you up here at six. We can have a drink, see the show and have dinner after. How does that sound!"

"Sounds wonderful to me. My last name is, Marrs, Janice Marrs."

9. The Crew

First days, anywhere, are always unique! Jac was really pumped! He had everything he would need, two pencils, a pen, six legal tablets (including the one with all the insurance company names, you never know when they might come in handy), nose drops (chronic case of allergy), Dentine for breath, two framed pictures of the planes he flew in the War, a framed copy of his Honorable Discharge and evidence of a Law degree. He was READY!

"Honey, Mr. Brooks wants to meet you"

"Missy, in private, call me, Jac. In public, call me Mr. Cartwright…please."

"Okay, Hun. Oh, I mean Jac."

Talk about surprises. First there was the outside of the building. Then there was the inside. And now, here was the Presidential office, to say the least! No Roebuck furniture here! The room had to have been decorated by an expert! Talk about your private offices. This one had everything for comfort…little for work. Jason Alfred Brooks was more than happy to show Jac everything! *Damask* drapery, velvet settee with matching love seats, ebony *credenza* and custom desk. Casual seating and end tables. *Had it not been for the Navy, he would never have been able to recognize any of the examples of 'elitist's avarice.'*

"My Boy, glad to have you aboard! There's a few things I want you to know about me. I only want people I can trust when I'm not here! When I'm here I always know what's happening! I'm what you call a 'hands-off manager,' if you can't do the job, I'll know about it soon enough. Emmery has been with me from our opening day, five years ago. He's like my second pair of eyes. And, Willy or Jinksy as he prefers to be called, has been here over four years. Hell, if you ever want to get his goat, just call him, Willy. It just gripes the shit out of him! It's always good for a laugh! I almost forgot! What's this crap about your name is Jacques, but you spell it, j-a-c, and you want people to call you j-a-c-k? Are you kidding? Was you mother frightened by a foreign dictionary?"

Jac ignored the question. "I have a question, Sir. You mentioned Whitehouse Insurance has been open five years, do you have your State Charter yet?"

"Great question, Kid! The five years will be up in three more months. And, this motley crew will have a celebration this town hasn't seen in years. It's going to be some 'deal to draw to!' Keep your nose to 'whatever the hell they call it' and you too, will be partying!"

"Thank you, Sir. I'm very happy be with you and the crew, and I hope I will make you proud of my work."

"Cut the crap! Do your job. Save me money, and, I'll be happy.!"

"Yes, Sir."

"That's enough of that, too; My name is Mr. Brooks."

Emmery Gant entered the room. *Jac was most thankful. He had the feeling there was more to Mr. Brooks than he needed to know at the moment. The only thing he needed was to be sure he kept himself 'clean.' Nothing sub-rosa, no under the table deals with anyone, especially, not with Mr. "save me money" Brooks. There was just something about him that made Jac's neck hairs curl.*

"Mr. Brooks, Mr. Cartwright and I have some important things to go over and I'd like start now."

Brooks dismissed the two men with a waved of a hand, while reaching for a decanter of bourbon.

"May I call you, Jac, when we are alone?

"Of, Course."

"Good. And, you call me, Em. Okay?"

Jac took notes as fast as he could. Em, was not short on breath. He spoke in 'chunks' of information, in a quick, choppy manner. In spite of the volume of information to share, 'share' was hardly an accurate description of the depth of his desire to communicate, Em knew the 'what,' and 'why things' happened in their little 'community.' More importantly, he knew where all bones were buried! With a lowered voice, he told Jac that Missy had an unhealthy habit of kissing and telling. Em, said he was sure it would mean her death some day. Soon, more likely than later. Em said Brooks made the mistake of taking her 'on,' in all meanings of the word. It only took a couple of days for Brooks to find out that she bragged about the tryst. At first, Em said he thought Brooks liked the idea of being a 'player' but, later it seemed that it began to bite him, especially when he applied to the Melrose Golf Club. There was some mention of decorum on the links at all times. "No interaction with the help." Brooks was furious! Em, wanted Jac to know about Brook's and Jinksey's illegal behavior, as he called it. When pressed to speak in nouns and verbs, no skidding around corners with the truth, he shared his suspicions about two off-shore accounts he happened to find (while ransacking Brook's 'private bookkeeping' journals) that combined, held some 1.3 million dollars. Jac asked him if he was sharing these things so Jac would do something about it or was he just indulging Jac as a way of becoming his confidant. Em never really stated his case clearly. *If nothing else, Jac could feel himself becoming less certain of the ethics being played both in and out in this company.* By comparison, according to Em, Jinksey was a 'small potato.' Slower to accumulate dollars, but no less effective than Brooks in 'covering.'

"So, let me see if I really understand what you just told me. Brooks has two off-shore accounts but no real information to directly connect him personally, right? And, Jinsksey, as head of Sales, is helping himself to some of the profits, correct? So, if I'm on the right track, suppose you tell me how he does it."

"Okay, in plain words. The Sales department sells auto insurance by cold calling, door-to-door, telephone, friends, or any other manner possible. The people pay a first month's payment. I register all monies collected. We send a list of newly insured to the State of California Insurance Commission monthly. The insured continue to send money to us and we send a portion of the monies to the State. It's like a contingence fund that makes sure monies will be available in the event of an accident claim. If you just left all the money with the insurance companies to hold, not spend, there would never be any money for the poor jerk who bought the insurance. Get it? Now, here's the good part. How does Jinksy get his cut, and I don't mean his salary? I'm talking cold cash. Every new insured sale is given to Jinksy to add to our list that is given to the State. He's a smart fellow. Good at cards. Great at math, and glib as hell! He says he can talk anyone out of suing the company. And, has, on several occasions. He holds back some of the new accounts, puts them into his bottom, desk drawer. That's having balls for you…his bottom, desk drawer! No key, no nothing! And every month he keeps the money sent in for "his" cases. God, that would make me crazy! He figures he might take a loss on a few of them, but his take is so big he can afford it, at least he thinks he can. So far, no problems. He said he clears about five grand a month and has for the last four years. And, I believe him."

Jac interrupt Emmery, "How is it that he told you about all of this illegal stuff? I'm really curious."

"Easy, he caught me with my hand in the cookie jar. Just peanuts compared to him."

"What the hell were you doing? Jeese, this gets better by the minute. Does this company really 'make' money? If it does, how does that happen? I'm I ever going to get paid?"

"Well, we probably have the greatest packages of any insurance company going. Not to mention, the greatest, to quote the boss, 'crew of salesmen.' They will do anything to make a sale. I've even heard some have done babysitting and laundry. Isn't that a kick! Anyway it works. Money for everybody This company is good for about one mil a month in new Apps alone, not to mention those monthly payments. Any more questions? I've got to get back to work."

"You were going to tell me what it is that you do to make a little extra."

"Well, my forte is bookkeeping. Any kind. Cooked or uncooked. I'm expert. You couldn't recognize one of my cooked-sets if your life depended on it."

"So, how did you get found out?"

"I was really stupid! My wife calls up, Jinksy answers my phone, in my office with me sitting there, she's telling him there's been a fire in our kitchen and I should come home. When I hear that, I go bezerk! And, I'm the one person in the entire company who NEVER loses his composure! I start yelling about the money in the wall. My 'hundred dollar hole' in the kitchen wall behind the stove! Naturally, Jinksy smells a con and wants to know all about it. I told him it was no big deal. It was just like saving pocket-change. A few extra bills from petty cash now and then. Or, change left over from trips to the post office. Or, say a small markup on postage weight; we have to send huge packets of information to the State and to the policy holders, and the like. Nothing big. Just pocket change. I tell him I wait until I have a hundred bucks. I get a hundred dollar bill, roll it in a tight roll and stick it into the small hole behind our kitchen stove. I tell him, 'that's why I went NUTS!' He's such a damn, smart ass, he tells me I'm stupid, small potatoes, too dumb 'to get it right,' and that he's the only genius in this operation! And, IF everything should ever go down, he said he will never be held to an accounting. He really pisses me off! There are times when I wish his stupid tennis-elbow would break, or something. He gets a lot of mileage in the form of time off from work. I'll bet he never spends more than five hours a week here. He only spends enough time to do his special bookkeeping.

Miss-bad-breath, entered Em's room without knocking. Smiling from ear to ear. "Glad to see the two of you get along so great. That's what makes a happy office."

"Don't you ever knock? Just because Brooks keep you here, did you ever figure out there is only one reason why? And, don't forget that I'm the office manager, I do what Brooks wants and he want me to keep an eye on you! That's the only reason you are still here. Get it?"

"Oh, Honey, don't trouble yourself, I'm here because, Brooksie wants me to keep an eye on you! How do you like them apples?" *With a flip of uncombed hair and a wicked-hip she leaves!*

"She just says that to get my goat."

"So, why give her so much power? Falling for that seems to leave a lot to be desired. Has it changed anything for you?" *Jac had always wanted to find an appropriate time to use the statement. It was something he'd once heard a Captain say.*

"Your office is going to be next to mine." Em had ignored everything Jac has said.

"Mr. Emmery is that so you can 'keep an eye on me?'"

"It's so I can keep an eye on both of you! By the way, how do you plan to split your time?"

"Since we are on Pacific Time, I thought you folks probably need to use East Coast information in the a.m. more than in the afternoon. That way, I could do my own work after lunch. Until I get going on my own work I am willing to do some extra for the company. It's going to a little time to get everything in place. Do you have any thoughts on changes?"

"Sounds, okay to me. It could become a real juggling act once you really get started. Until now, we been going 'out' for legal advice. We have our own lawyers who do our trial work. We don't have many trials. Less than most companies because our payout record is pretty good. As Brooks is wont to say 'I don't like to dick around much, so just take care of it!' Simple translation, screw'm or pay if you have to."

Extending his hand, Jac, said, "Well, this has been more than I could have imagined! You have been a fount of information, I'm not sure what you want me to do with it, but you know I have to keep your confidentiality, so no worries. Not from me, anyway. I don't suggest you share much of this with anyone else. It could come back to bite all of you folks. Enough said! I'd like to see my office."

What a surprise! Two chairs, one leather in dark maroon, to match the beautiful desk (one of two in the room), a desk-set, gold pen and all, clock in the middle; two large, colorful prints on the wall, telephone on the desk extension, and a secretary *at the ready* by her desk. Everything flanked by rows and rows of law books! God, what a perfect set-up! *I can't wait to tell Janice all about this!*

"So, what do you think, Kid?" Brook's booming voice made Jac flinch. "You know why this looks like it does? Simple, the people you are going to have to take care of have to think you are hot stuff and are getting paid a bunch! All window dressing! Don't let it go to your head. Got it? *"Got it?" Seemed to be a favorite question in LA.. At least at Whitehouse Insurance.*

"I'm really impressed, Mr. Brooks. I won't forget what you said."

"Good, Boy! That's what I like to hear. Keep it up and you'll be in for a good raise!"

When it came to money, Jac would be receiving more than he ever dreamed. Without all the extras, he would be getting a salary of $300 a month. $300 was what most fledgling attorneys would be making for working for a company all day, much less free use of the office for any personal phones calls. Jac could hardly contain himself. His mind was in full tilt with all the things he knew he could accomplish if only given the opportunity. AND, THE OPPORTUNITY WAS HERE!

"Missy, let's you and I set-up a schedule for the two of us. I have an idea about the kind of phone log I want to keep. There is also the issue of confidentiality when clients come into this office. I noticed there was little in the way real privacy in any of the other offices, but we can't have that happening here. We need a wall between us, with a door of course, when people want to speak with me."

"Brooksie will never go for it, hon."

"I guess it will have to be his choice; me or a wall!"

"You don't really mean that!"

Within an hour Em came into Jac's office. "I explained everything to Brooks, about how it was 'what you needed,' not what you wanted, and he said the guys would have it built before you came in Monday. I don't know how, but you are in good with the Big Man, he likes you. Lucky you!"

"Em, come in for a minute. I want to bounce a couple of things off you. First, how are we going to handle supplies? I'm going to need quite a few at the beginning. I will need to know that I can trust you not to take a 'few cents here and a few cents there' from my requisitions. I just don't EVER want to have to discuss why some 'cents' are missing. Understood?"

"Not to worry."

"Good. I will also need your advice about Company Policy; regulations, restrictions, and the like from time to time, since I'm new to auto insurance. In return, I will be available to you in a professional way should you ever have, and I'm sure you will, need my help. Sound, okay? Now for the more important ramifications of our relationship. I watch your six, I mean back, and you watch mine. Does that sound Equitable? *Em nods.* I will want to meet Mr. Jinkouski when he comes in next time. I need to know my cohorts. What you folks do reflects on me. And, I'm not too happy about what I've heard so far. From what I've been told, having a 6800 Wilshire Boulevard address can't hurt, so I'm depending on you to work with me. I can foresee my using you in a professional way. How would you like to become my investigator later on? I think you would be great!

"You can count on me, Jac! I'm with you all the way. Who knows, I may get used to being 'legal'…or not. But, I think so, it's just a new concept right now. You know, if you ever leave here and get your own office, you may want to take me with you. Right? That would be a real kick! Me gone straight! What a concept! I'm really an okay fellow, Jac. It's just that I've been around such jerks that it almost begs to become a con job. I mean look at Brooks. Have you ever met a guy more ready to be plucked?"

"You know, Em, I look at people differently from you. No criticism intended. Where I come from, people had such a hard time, living hand to mouth, and doing whatever it took to feed a family that we had little time to think of doing anything underhanded to a neighbor. I hate to say it, but if the War hadn't come along, God knows where any of us would be today! I never saw a checkbook until I was in Law school. And, Law school only came because of the GI Bill. Yes, I served my Country, and my Country continues to serve me. It's been the best of all times for me. Not for all who served with me…but never got …back. I'm just thankful that I was smart enough to know that we would be in the War and that I decided I wanted to 'ride not walk,' that's why I became a pilot. God help me, so many didn't make it."

"Oh."

"I'm sorry, Em, why did you let me go on and on, I didn't mean to bore you to death! God, I'm Really sorry!"*The look in Em's face made him feel like a heel.* "It just hits me every so often. The Gospel truth is I could very well be back shucking corn off the Mississippi; were it not for the War!"

Jac had vivid memories, some hurtful, others humorous, of the Great Depression. One of the major problems of growing up in rural areas before WWII was apathy. Not so much with those who had acreage, like Jac's folks, a good 80 acres of bottom land with tenant farmers, but those who were the tenants. There are many more tenants, eleven to one, than land owners. "Land owners" has a nice ring to it, but meant very little in financial terms!

Tenants' meant that many families decided land was the only way to survive in the country. Good thought. Not particularly rational when they had to provide the tools, food, fodder, and incentive for tenant-farmer survival. Thankfully, education was a valued premium in Jac's home. Mother had earned a teaching degree from Normal College, and had taught for two years before it giving-up. The kids were bigger and older than she. The truth … she hated them!

In spite of her teaching experiences, Jac's mother was a very tolerant person at home. Jac wasn't sure it was true tolerance, it could have been her resistance to confrontation. Example, the time Jac's sister thought she was grown-up enough to do whatever she wanted to do. She tried smoking in the downstairs bathroom thinking she was alone. Aunt Bernice's balding-boyfriend, was to drive the two sisters to Devon. Before leaving, mom realized she had left her glasses in the bathroom. She opened the door, cleared the heavy smoke from in front of her, and said goodnight to my sis before closing the door. Nothing more. Dad would have had a hissy! We would have heard about it for a month! On a good side, his attitude on education was, "You only get one time to learn and If you don't get top grades…don't come home!" Jac knew he meant every word. The threat had its benefits.

Tenant farmers as a general rule believed their kids had the responsibility of caring for their families by continuing to farm. Often the children exhibited little respect for self or others. Many times Jac witnessed the sickening abuse heaped on a mother by both the dad and the kids; Hitting, kicking, name calling, spitting! Really disgusting! You could never tell if the abuse was as a result of the depressed times or, being from humble, but ignorant beginnings.

Jac's dad wasn't abusive in the same way. But, he did things almost as bad. Days upon days, ignoring everyone in the house. Spending his time trying to 'square a sphere! ' Or, arguing politics with any crony who happened to stop. The grand joke of it all, was the fact the dad had never voted! He had special responses for a fist full of activities that other people share as ordinary. He seemed to enjoy swearing when he couldn't think of anything else to say. Occasionally, he threw food on the floor when it didn't suit his taste. Tying a kid up or slapping was about as physical as it got. Gramma Diffy set the limit! Fortunately, Jac did not subsume the ignorant behavior of his father. Intelligent, was how the family used to think about the father who always had got the last word. Now, Jac was not so sure. Jac knew he needed to be different!

Some of the good memories he had about the depression where of times he would stop in the grocery store and listen to the little four-tube radio that was always playing music. Or, longingly look at the old punch board resting against the cash register, He would dream of how he would spend the money. Jac often wondered how many winners there been in the life of the ' Win A Five Dollar Bill' card. The grocer was a strange fellow. Some kind of foreigner. He was always friendly enough. He often gave Jac an Abbazzabba bar, which was one of Jac's favorites. It had a kind of chewy outside with some peanut butter in the middle, which made it Jac's favorite treat.

Mr. Schmuck, the grocer, wasn't the only foreigner in town. Jack's father opined that Schmuck must be a German because the local paper had been reporting on the 'German Schmucks' for well over 100 years and were apparently one of the first groups of foreigners to seek out the Bottom Lands. In a town of fewer than 2000 people, there was something akin to a colonial grouping of people; Some German, another Scotch, some Irish, and others English. The town had its own newspaper most of it was dedicated to the column titled '100 years ago.' Even as a child Jac used to laugh, thinking that the only thing that would ever happen in his town would have to be 100 years old before it could be reported. To Jac, most of the folks looked 100 years old.

There were some good times. Those were the times when Jac would take Shep, and the two of them would go down to the creek. Jac, ostensibly looking for geodes his dad could sell, and Shep looking for rabbits. Jac always took his gun. It was a gift from uncle Ed, one of two relatives Jac really loved. Going to the river was a chance to get away from the tension in the summer house. There were many snippets of time when Jac had the opportunity to explore the natural beauty that surrounded him. With thanks to his mother, Jac took the time to differentiate color as his surroundings changed one season to another. Jac often thought his mother might have developed an artistic talent given the opportunity. And, who knows, perhaps dad could have become the mathematician he always believed he was. There were no bread lines in Jac's town. There weren't any negro people either except for one. He was the school janitor. The janitor and his family tended to keep to themselves. Thinking back on it, Jac, thought it rather strange that he had never heard a single derogatory remark made about any member of the janitor's family, even though the Ku Klux Klan was still quite active in parts of Illinois. Fortunately, no one in Jack's family condoned Klan activity. Jac was glad that he had grown up in a gentler, less radical and rambunctious family.' Except for dad, of course. There were a couple of important disadvantages; You didn't really know what was happening around you, much less in the Country. A good thing was you didn't really know that you were poor, everyone looked the same, dressed the same, ate the same food, and engaged in the same disagreements; most of a political nature. The only difference amongst neighbors was the heights to which some would propel their grievances. Some ending in court, others ending in the hospital, or worse the morgue.

Jac was determined to be a person who 'cared.' Jac needed to care about himself, and wanted to care for others, especially his family. He just didn't know where to start. He often wondered how people learned to give and accept love other than from one's own relations. He was pretty sure he loved his mother. He knew she loved him. He wasn't too sure of much else. He had decided to start with the few things he knew how to do. "I'm not afraid of work! I feel uncomfortable about being alone. But, I'm willing, in spite of a few niggling fears, to follow the 'plan.' And, God help me, I will succeed! But how do I start?"

∽

10. The Date

The well-dressed young man asked the cabby to wait."Am I on time?" Jac looked very nervous.

"You know you are. To be accurate, you are ten minutes early! You don't give a girl much of a chance!'

"Okay, you found me out. Is the date off?"

"Where have you been, my Dear? How is it that you are so damn sensitive? Can't you tell when a female is kidding?"

"Okay. Let's start again. Hi, Janice, great to see you! The taxi is waiting!"

"Don't you have a car?"

"No, car. Does that make a difference?"

"Should it?"

"What's happening? I'm confused! Again, I'm asking, is…the…date…off?"

Janice tippy-toed, deposited a soft kiss on his cheek.

"Does it look like it it's off?"

"Guess Not. See you when you come out!"

The evening was much too much to recall in detail. Red Shoes was sold out! So they did the next best. Janice suggested that they go to the Patriotic Hall and see a school chum of hers who was playing the part of the slave girl, Tondalayo, in White Cargo. The stage performance was considerably more 'earthy' than Jac was accustomed to. If truth be told, Jac thought the best part of the evening was when they stopped at Tiny Naylor's coffee shop for pie and coffee. Jac was learning that everything of importance was on Wilshire Boulevard. Tiny's was open all night so that gave them plenty of time to share hopes and dreams. Jac, was confident he would not relax until he had became a 'trial lawyer of considerable note!' He shared how he wanted his father to live to see it happen! Janice, on the other hand, wanted to finish (in truth) continue what she considered a real education, not a War time excuse for what passed as education! 'Learn it fast! Do it fast! And, forget about the mistakes!' She planned to finish College and continue school with work, if possible. She was in full accord with Jac's plan; work hard, and build a meaningful future!

The night had been magic for Jac! Everything was new to him! He thought he did okay. But, now, it was time to say, good night! And, that's just what he said as he opened the door of the cab, "Hope you had a good time. Will I see you tomorrow night? I hope so. Good night." Janice laughed as she fled the cab. She was afraid she would ruin everything if she said any-thing. *He was just too good to be true. But he could be trained! He was not only a real gentleman, he was someone to respect…and 'retain!*

∽

11. Saturday In LA

JAC wasn't much for sleeping-in, especially not Saturday mornings. *The Y is a great place to stay but I'm going to find myself an apartment today even if it's only a one-room walk-up. I think I had better buy myself a small car too, not too big, just enough to take me around town. I wonder where they hide the gas stations around here? Hell, it doesn't matter I have all day to do it. Hot shower and some breakfast is certainly in order. And before I forget, I better do something about putting the rest of my money into bank since I've written the folks for some of the money I sent home. The Service was a perfect place to save money! First things, first! Call Janice.*

"Hi, Janice how about some breakfast? In return, you can help me buy car and find an apartment. I feel like a damn fool trying to do that by myself. I don't really know the area and you seem to have a good handle on it."

"You really surprise me Jac I didn't think I'd hear from you so soon. You said, see you tonight. And, I have to admit you seemed a little preoccupied last night, or was it just my scintillating personality?"

"I'm so sorry! It's just that I was so overwhelmed with all that had happened during the day, new job, great money, wonderful office, and more importantly, a new friend. It was just too much 'for a poor country boy.' Do you mind if I call you my friend?"

"Not that's all! How about that breakfast you promised me? There's a terrific place, Ollie Hammond's. On 'Wilshire'… of course! I want to take you there for breakfast, I'll pick you up in my car. Better give me your address again. I need about thirty more minutes, is that okay with you?"

The second cup of coffee gave the two of them plenty of time to talk about what they would be doing the rest of the day. Janice wanted very much to introduce Jac to a couple of neighborhoods that she felt would be in keeping with Jac's 'new position.' she laughed when he mentioned his willingness to 'take a walk-up.'

"Jac we don't have walk-ups in this town."

"Well, whatever you call them, I need something that's not too far from work. And, not too expensive."

"I think I have the perfect solution for you. It's called Lafayette Park Place, right off Wilshire Boulevard not too far from your work, probably no more than 2 or 3 miles. They're grand old apartments, most of them have rooms for rent. The address would be perfect for an attorney like yourself!"

"Believe it or not Janice I'm not used to the notion of being an attorney…yet. I'm still a guy that comes from a very small town. I hope it doesn't take me too long to get up to snuff. My dad always used to say that I was always day late and a dollar shorted."

"You're in LA now, my friend. You think you can put all those country notions to bed, and get with the plan? I'm going to scan the paper and when I mark what I believe to be appropriate lodging for you I'll give it to you and you can make your selection, okay?"

Jack couldn't help noticing how efficient Janice was. She came prepared. She had a copy of the Daily News, a pencil, note pad, an LA map and small scissors. For the next ten or fifteen minutes she was busy looking at and discarding potential addresses. Jac was intrigued as he watched Janice work. She attacked her work like a surgeon. she carefully noted distance, approximate travel time, and the probability of public transportation for each of the twenty-some locations. Jac hated to admit it but it was good to have someone helping him, it wasn't until he arrived in Los Angeles that he realized how much he depended on having someone around. He had to admit he felt a little embarrassed at the thought of an almost thirty-year old needing someone to be with him. So much for concerns, he remembered what Granny Diffy used to say' a person should never look a gift horse in the mouth!' And, Jac, most definitely, was not about to do that; not when he had a beautiful young woman to show him around town and, hopefully, help him get settled.

"I think we are ready to attack our list. I didn't realize I had so many 'possibles.' I'll pare them down to three or four."

They had just finished number three on the list; It was Lafayette Park Place, with a beautiful, old three-story. The room had not offered what Jac needed. The place was very old, dark, and had the unmistakable odor of eucalyptus oil and rubbing alcohol. It was too similar to being back home.

"After the last one, this looks like a good place, Jac, let me do the talking." This new location, just a block and a half north of Wilshire on Third Street looked like it had good potential. The apartment buildings, about thirty of them all looked alike, they looked very well-built, probably just before the War. Everything looked sparkling clean. The landlady of the selected address was like a character out of Dickens. She was about 6 feet tall with unkempt red hair, a sexy, black dress covered by a calico apron and gloves on both hands. She led them into a small, neat apartment that had a Murphy bed, a very tiny kitchen, with a hot plate and small refrigerator. The bathroom was incredible...and clean but, 'incredible' in that the landlady had cut out a huge, linoleum tree with orange fruit, ostensibly oranges, and pasted it onto the black, high-gloss wall next to the tub; festooned with free-flying, papier-mâché parrots hanging from the ceiling. The landlady offered that at one time the folks upstairs were going to take the apartment but they laugh when they saw the bathroom, they called it by some strange name, some foreign name she couldn't understand because they were either 'Japs or Jews.'

At least, the place smelled clean. Jac was happy to find out that everything was provided, the bedding, dishes, forks, spoons, pans. Everything included, and as Jac was to learn later, it also included absolutely no regard for OPA ceiling prices for apartments. [A government agency to insure that returning service personal would not be overcharged for rentals] In addition to the seven dollars a week advertised as the rent, the landlady collected an additional $125 a month. Janice told Jac she wasn't surprised because almost everyone was doing that; it was called getting-a- little more under -the-table. And, if you wanted a decent place to live you would have to 'go-along.' Jac didn't feel too badly about it since his $300 a month income was going to be more than enough, and he would soon be receiving the allotment money from his folks. In truth, $125 did rankled his 'attorney soul!' The Landlady, hardly a lady, since it was well known to the *establishment she had been a Madam during the war. Janice explained, that most of the apartments on 3rd St. had been brothels during the War and that the girls had moved on but the Madams remained as landlords.*

"If you still want to get a car I know a great place. It's at 35th and Grand. You'll love the guy who owns it! He advertizes as 'Cal Worthington and His Dog, Spot!' Only, Spot is a real tiger as are the other wild animals he uses in his ads. He's such an active character I wouldn't be surprised he lives to be a hundred! So tell me, should we eat, or go shop for cars?"

Jac felt like a newly, freed spirit! "I'm game for whatever! Remind me, when we go to dinner, I have an awesome idea for the two of us! He paused. "What would you think if I asked you to leave the Tick Tock and come work in my office?"

"You're either hungry or nuts! But I have to admit I am willing to listen."

"Okay, we get a car, 'on time,' I don't want to spend all of my money today. Then we can go where ever you say for a fantastic steak dinner. *Jac catches himself.* I'm sorry I should have asked you if you like steak."

"And, me from Kansas! What do you think? Although I have been known to try strange and sticky food in the past."

Jac wasn't paying much attention to what was being said, "It may sound crazy to you, but I think we would work well together in the same office. I wouldn't be your boss, but I would be able to protect you from all the men who would love to have a beautiful woman around! What do you say? Don't answer until you hear what I have in mind. You could say I'm planning a 'crap shoot.' Not anything akin to what I've ever been known to do."

"I can't say I like the sound of that! And, may I ask…did you hear anything I just said?"

"Of course, I did! What do you think I am?"

"Okay, what did I say?"

"You didn't like that I said 'crap shoot.' Just wait until I have an opportunity to explain, I think you will be as intrigued as I am. The Company is a cacophony of voices, much like six or seven trains, each on a separate track speeding head-long toward the station, only to meet on the same track."

Janice decided to let his tendency to ignore others pass. "Are you really serious about working with you?"

"yes!"

"So what do you plan for the two of us to accomplish, and how can we go about actually doing it? That sounds rather stupid. I speak as though I had some, or any idea of what you have in mind!"

"Understood! Let's get the car before it gets dark. I'd like to be able to see what I'm getting."

Getting the car was a snap! Janice made it painless. He was now the proud owner of a 'previously owned automobile' and, according to all accounts, a few knocks and squeals were nothing to worry about! He would pick up the car tomorrow; he refused to take a dirty car. Janice suggested they eat now, and of course, knew just the place! The meal at Laurie's Prime Rib was phenomenal as far as Jac was concerned! He had never eaten a more perfect steak in his life. Very few of these in Warsaw! The greatest surprise was to learn that the finest eateries in all of Los Angeles were located on San Vicente Boulevard which was the side street to his new office!

"Didn't you happen to see any of the restaurants when you went out to lunch yesterday?"

"No, I just crossed the street to a little sandwich shop."

"You must mean Nathan's brother's shop. I think it's called Abe's Deli."

"You're right! That's the one."

"What did you eat?"

"Just Ham on rye and a glass of milk."

Janice broke into convulsive laughter.

"What's so funny about a ham on rye, I don't get it!"

"Sorry, it won't happen again. Jac, it was a Jewish deli!"

"So?"

"Didn't you have any Jews in your town? At least, where you went to Law school."

"I don't know, I never asked."

"By the way where did you go to Law school?"

"Well, are you ready for this, Topeka, Kansas!"

"You've got to be kidding!"

"I'm not. I really would like to know how a girl from Kansas, who eats beef, knows EVERYTHING about a city the size of LA!"

"Simple. I was far more unsure of my decision to go 'west' then you. I didn't have a big education to take me through the lonely nights, so I spent most of my time pouring over travel guides and maps; LA, Hollywood *Home of The Stars*, Santa Monica, Malibu where the Stars live, and The Miracle Mile! *She gave Jac a huge smile.* "I'm kind 'a glad I did." *She was always a 'quick' study and could manage a 'cover story' on the spot! She was certain Jac was none the wiser.*

Jac ignored her obvious advance, "Well, I think it's too late to go anywhere. Do you agree?"

"It's much too late to go some place and have to become active! I'm still too full. How about you?"

"That's what I was thinking. How about a slow stroll down the boulevard?"

"Suppose you just place yourself into my care for the hour or so, and I'll give you the show of your life! By the way, have you seen the ocean yet?"

"No. I've only been here a few days. Is that going to be the show?"

"Place yourself in my hands, remember? No questions!"

Janice turned her car around and drove to Wilshire and Sunset. There was the usual crush of cars in both directions. She waited for a break in the traffic and quickly turned into a garishly-lit, motel driveway. Nothing the likes of anything Jac had ever seen before! He could only bring himself to say aloud, "If you've got the money, Honey, I've got the time!" Janice Ignored him and backed out of the driveway and pulled forward so she could take a parking place, with a better view of the Pacific. Jac could feel the heat of his embarrassment rising through the limbs, who momentarily, felt the heat of unexpected excitement! The view was exceptional! The red tide and phosphorescence added an element of beauty! The waves were awash with the colors of a rainbow.

Jac was at a loss for appropriate words. The best he could manage was, "Unfortunately, my dad said all things connected with the ocean, manmade or natural, were associated with evil. He dared me to find any reference to a ship, or large body of water that wasn't called, or referred to as 'she' plus the Bible said a 'she' was the evil one; dad may have been literarily correct, but I detested the association."

"Just small town, remember?" Janice gave his leg a pat.

"By the way, which town did you hail from, Janice?"?"

"The outskirts of Kansas City. No big excitement! Just more work."

"Which was?"

"You are asking a lot of questions for a person too tired to 'do anything.' *Laughing, she caught him short.* Oh, yah, I forgot, you're an *A..TTORNEY!* They always ask questions."

"Are you making fun of me?" *He began tickling her ribs. She was ticklish, but jac realized he was acting like a dumb grammar school kid at recess.*

"Look, Friend, I'm the kind of girl that deals with direct information; if rib-tickling is one of your ways of performing fore-play, you need to let me know in advance. I'm no good at guessing."

Again, Jac was so embarrassed he couldn't speak. The silence became a leaden-blanket over the two of them.

Janice asked, "What do you say, I just drive you home?"

"NO!" *Jac left absolutely no question that he meant 'NO!'* "I need to talk to you. Look, I'm just a dumb cluck who doesn't have much experience around women. Too busy in the War, too busy in school, too removed from my sister, and afraid to get too near my mother. I guess I'm playing it by the wrong ear."

"Then…do us both a favor Jac, don't try to be clever. I get it, you don't think I do, but I do get it! I think what you're trying to say, is that right now everything is in the jumble. In the last 24 hours your life has been turned upside down. New town, new job, new car, and a woman you think is coming on to you. Well, maybe I was in a way. Suffice it to say, you need some time. There is absolutely no rush as far as I'm concerned. How about if I take you to a spot that begs for a little attention and a lot of money!."

"Thanks for the kind words and understanding, Janice. As for the special spot, you have my full attention and unbridled curiosity. Are you sure it's not too late, you said you had to work tomorrow."

"Well, did you mean what you said about working with you? If you did, I'll just call in sick. I can't tell you how badly I wanted to leave that place. My folks would die if they knew I'd been working in a bar. So, as for it being late, both of us can sleep late."

Jack felt his body's nervous response at the thought of, even the slimmest possibility of, the two of them sleeping in the same bed. You are one stupid fool my friend! Get a grip!" Jac rarely missed an opportunity to emasculate himself.

Janice drove in silence as her little car struggled to make one hill after another on a two-lane road that became Mulholland drive. The 'best place in all of the County' to view the entire San Fernando Valley!

"Janice, I can't see a thing it's too dark!"

"That's why they say this is the best 'make-out' place in the State. Sorry, that's a wrong impression, Jac. I didn't bring you here to make-out. I brought you here to tell you of some of the plans I have for my future. You may not be able to see the valley, but I can tell you all about the opportunities it offers. Right now it's miles and miles and miles of orange, grapefruit and lemon trees; dotted here and there with ranches, not cattle, mostly horses. My understanding is, most of the ranches are owned by movie folks. No big deal as far as I'm concerned. I did take the time to do a little investigating. I can buy a strip of land, one acre wide, between Raven and Saticoy, boarded on the West by Reseda Boulevard for only $2,500. Someone described it as a 'steal. Play your cards right and you too might become a land baron! I know it's too dark to see anything; just wait until I have a chance to bring you back!"

"That's all well and good, but it sounds like most of the national debt to me."

"Well, you wouldn't think so if you had chatted with one of my rare, but well known, after-theater customers. He came into the Tick a couple of months ago. When he was all alone, I asked him if he would like to sit at the bar and we could keep each other company. He had my full attention for at least three hours, telling me about Coldwell Banker, Mr. Whitsitt and a couple other friends that wanted him to invest in the Valley. He even gave me the name of a realtor he trusted. He said I'd be a rich woman if I got just a small piece of land. He told me about a builder who 'bulldogged' his way into one of the investor's office and convinced him to provide the money for a 'vision.' He said the realtor the man had a plan that was a win, win situation! Everyone would get rich! After all, the US Government would 'front' the money for these Housing Units for Veterans! He said he personally had to do a lot of talking in order to ramrod the idea through the powers that be, but if I took a good look at what was happening I would have a front seat at what would no doubt become one of the largest building contracts in the County! Alden Builders were prepared to build several thousand homes for vets. Now I'm fin- ished! So... what do you think about my idea?" *Janice had accomplished everything she was assigned to do; and then some! She could tell Jac was more than just 'a little' interested. This however, was one of the times she regretted working on a new recruit for the Agency!*

Sporting a huge smile, Jac responded, "I think you are the perfect woman to have around! You couldn't possibly know what it means to me to hear a woman speak with conviction in her voice. One thing for sure lady, you've given me a caseload to think about. I don't want to spoil the mood but I'm hungry again! It must be the night air."

"Where do you want to eat? We'll have to try and find something open all night. My poor, little puddle- Jumper, doesn't like Sepulveda Pass very much... too many hills. I'm glad it's a little cooler tonight; my car hasn't heated up even once."

"If you promise not to take me wrong,. we could find an all-night store, buy some eggs, milk, bread and butter and "I could'a cooka for you...a ...my 'spe-cial-ity!' Scram-boola eggs! At-a my-a... new housa. Don't laugh. I know, my accent is lousy, but I did make an effort to perk up a little bit."

"Terrific! Janice gave his knee a slap, "We can make a night of it! After all this could be the very last time either one of us will have the opportunity of just letting it 'all the parts fall where they may' as the kids say. I'm game! Let's just be a couple of goofy kids after high school prom. We'll go and do whatever we want and we won't report to a single person! God, I haven't let myself go this much in an age! I can't remember the last time I just had fun! Thanks, Fella! By the way, I thought you said your mother was Irish. Your Italian is wonderful."

"There's really not much difference. My service buddies taught me all Europeans are Europeans, and folks from the United Kingdom are much the same as the Italians when it come to family behavior; or so they said. And, you don't have to thank me for my sad interpretation! I think your idea is great! It's so late I don't know what else we can do." *Jac hoped he had 'covered' growing inner sense of panic and excite-ment. The thought of having her alone in his apart-ment was a little more than he wanted to think of... at the moment.* "Just going to let the chips fall where they may." *Jac never realized how promising his father's well-worn mantra could have been all these years.*

"Here it is, good old Safeway, you can always count on the store to be open. Did you know they offer people who have house-cars the opportunity to park in their parking lot all night free of charge? I'd say that's a good example of the good old American Spirit!"

"I didn't realize the store was so close to my apartment. What's the name of this street?"

"Rampart."

Fortuitously, Janice had selected some paper plates and Styrofoam cups so there wasn't much trash to take care of. The too 'high school kids' stretched out, chins on palm's, on top of the Murphy bed.

"It's been a glorious time for me Jac! I don't know how I can never thank you for picking up my spirits and giving me a chance to smile and laugh. I didn't realize how depressed I've been working in the bar. I know I put up a pretty good front, but it's all underneath, had you not come in when you did, I probably would have been there for years. *Liar! Liar!* The most daring thing I've done since I've been in LA was to take that drive to the San Fernando Valley and look at property. Honestly, I don't expect you to get all het up about it."

"Don't count me out so quickly. I'm in for a good plan as well as anyone else, at the moment I need to concentrate on getting a better apartment; there just isn't room here for much more than my own big feet. I'm guessing this whole place can't be more than 225 square feet. I think they did a terrific job fitting

67

everything in its place. I have to admit I've never seen one of these beds that come out of the wall." *Jac had been so busy thinking about his apartment he hadn't noticed that Janice had fallen asleep. He carefully folded one of the blankets over her, slipped off his shoes, placed a pillow between them, and fell fast asleep.*

There was a loud continuous banging at the front door! The landlady's voice could have been heard blocks away. "There is one thing I will not tolerate in my apartment! No one is allowed to hoar around in these rooms! Cartwright, if you intend to live here... you live alone! You told me you were not married so get that slut out of your apartment! Do it now!"

Jack had opened the door fully clothed, in the middle of her tirade, "If you come in I think you'll be able to see that no one has been, to use your words 'hoaring' around! By the way how did you know she was even here?"

"You said you didn't own a car and I saw the two of you pull up in a car last night and come into the building."

"I don't wish to disagree, but it was hardly last night, it was more like this morning. Do you stay up all night watching who comes and goes. As a new tenant, I'd like I give you a bit of advice. Litigation is very costly, and I'm positive you hadn't even thought of the ramifications when you so brazenly, banged on MY door. I know you will never do it again because if you do I will take you to court and it won't cost me a cent! Good morning to you!"

"Boy, you slam doors really well! When did I fall asleep; the last thing I remember you were planning to get another apartment."

"You're right, it was about that time. I think the two of us are just a couple of Piker's when you come right down to it. Are you up to taking me for a little ride before I pick up my car? I'd like to show you my office and if I'm lucky I might be able to meet the elusive "Mr. Jinkowski." Emmery said he usually comes in on Sunday."

"I think I look too frazzled to meet anyone. Would you mind if we stopped at my apartment just long enough for me to freshen up a bit and put on some different clothes?"

"I think you look terrific just the way you are, but will do whatever you want."

Janice really appreciated those kind words. She wasn't accustomed to hearing them, she felt secure in the knowledge that they would first become friends ...'after that, who knows.' Even if she wasn't allow to be straight with Jac at the present time; if all went well, they would truly be working together in **the Agency**.'

12. Sunday Office Visit

Jac didn't hear a thing as he unlocked the huge front doors. He hoped the carpenters would be working on his *confidentiality* wall. No such luck, no workman, no nothing. Jac led Janice into his room. He felt a flicker of personal pride as Janice validated the presence of beautiful furnishings.

"Boy did you hit a jackpot!"

"My sentiments exactly." They had just seated themselves when they heard the large downstairs door slam shut.

"Maybe it's the carpenters, I hope so."

"I don't hear anyone do you, Jac?"

"No, I don't... that's strange. I think I'll investigate, you stay here."

"No thank you sir, I'm going with you!"

That's when they heard the sound of the drill. The sound was coming from the end of the hallway. It sounded as though it came from Mr. Brook's office. Jac and Janice quietly crept toward the office, but stopped quickly when they heard a litany of swear words, many of which, neither had ever heard before!

"You, God damn, no good, cock-sucking, evil son of a bitch!' Brooks was in shock. He literally ran into the two of them in the hallway nearly falling into their arms. Through half-closed eyes, he mumbled, "What the Blue Jesus are you doing here on Sunday?"

Janice was the first to notice Brooks left arm was bleeding profusely. "Looks like he cut an artery! Here, give me a hand, I need something to stop the bleed-ing! Jac take off your tie, I'll buy you a new one!" Both Jac and Brooks were stunned as they watched Jan-ice, deftly stem the flow of blood with two quick wraps of the tie around the forearm, then lead Brooks to a chair.

Jac asked in a clear, loud tone, "What in Blue Blazes were you doing in your office?"

Without waiting for an answer, Janice said they needed to get him to an emergency room, *right now*! Jac thought better of it, considering Brooks' tremen-dous size. He stayed with Brooks while Janice called for an ambulance.

Brook's last words to the two of them were, "And, stay out of my office!" He passed out as they wheeled him into the ambulance.

"That was rather strange wouldn't you say? Now…I really want to go inside that office! Are you going to come with me Jac?"

Neither one could believe their eyes! Brooks had been using a 36 inch, one-inch bore, concrete drill. It must have hit something unexpectedly, which caused it to jump and in turn caused the gash on Brook's forearm.

"What do you suppose he was trying to do?" Jac, asked incredulously.

"Easy. He's trying to make a bigger hole so he can watch the people down below. Look over here, on this side of his chair. There's another hole that is much smaller."

Jac had to think for a moment. When he entered the building he thought the reception area in compassed the entire area of the second floor. No small mezzanine. Not true. There WAS yet a smaller, but compact section of working cubicles below the three offices: Brook's, Em's and his own office! "What the hotel bill is going on here? This place is a genuine enigma! We had better leave."

Janice gave Jac a huge smile as she reached to give him a little kiss on the cheek. "You my friend are one, cute fellow without a tie! What say we go pick-up your car?"

෬෩

13. On The Job

The office was buzzing when Jac entered the second floor corridor. People were mentioning 'Jac' in the same breath with 'hero' and 'newcomer.'

Missy greeted him with a huge hug! "You're the bravest man I know. I'm so lucky to be working for such a good-looking guy. And, a hero, no less!"

Just the sound of her voice made him miss Janice all the more! He told Janice to come over about 11 o'clock so he could introduce her to Em. He was sure Em would find something for her, after all she'd been the one who had actually saved the old Puttz! *Spying on his employees! Who ever heard of such a thing?*

"It's time to go to work Missy! I want you to bring a list of all the files that outside attorneys are handling. Between the two of us, I believe we can shake a few things up around here. That is, you will have to be on time every morning. I noticed you were about 40 minutes late. I want both of us to work with the same ethic. Forty minutes late in the morning means forty minutes more At the end of the day."

"You're kidding, right"

"Wrong!"

Just then Janice entered his office, her timing was impeccable! True she was early for her appointment, but jac the needed the interruption! He didn't think he could take another moment of, Missy!"

"Boy, am I glad to see you!" He threw his arms around her, surprising both of them. *That felt pretty good. I'll have to try that one again soon. I'm proud of you my man, that was a good move; I'm sure you can manage to do that again...right?*

Jac brought Janice to Em's this office. Em jumped from his chair and hurried to embrace Jac. *Jac didn't know Em could move that fast.*

"My God Jac, what would have happened if you hadn't s saved that guys life? My whole deal would have been down the crapper! I felt sick when I heard how close it had come! Anything I can do for you! Anything! Just name it!"

"You will never know how glad I am you asked! It gives me great pleasure to present to you, Ms. Janice Marrs. Hopefully, she will become my new secretary. Em, like I told you I really want to be a team player, it's just that Missy is more than I can stand! Please! I'll never ask you for another thing."

"Consider it done. I'll be glad to take 'wiggler' back into my office. She has her moments but they all lack decorum. I had told Brooks she wasn't right for your office, but would he listened... 'no dice!' Thanks for bolstering my side of this miserable denominator."

The Student and the Teacher hugged again when they got back to Jac's office, this time Jac knew how!

"Are you going to tell Em about the hole in the floor? And, by the way...the hug felt great!"

"Absolutely, I'll tell him when we're alone. That reminds me, what happened to the workmen that were supposed to build this *confidentiality* wall? Brooks must have just been blowing smoke. We'll see. Look, I know you have never been a secretary. No matter. I'm going to buy a dictating machine for both of us. Besides, I type quite well. I had to learn for law school. No typing for you, I'll want you to answer the phone and taking messages. When you feel like it, you can put together a client list for me. I will really appreciate it if you will keep your ear opened when you go to the water cooler. That's where all the dirt is passed, according to Em. I need to know if this is going to be a safe environment for my first law practice. I, for sure, don't want to be caught in anybody else's mess that could jeopardize my license to practice." *Jac went to her (a brazen move for him), gave her a hug, and kissed her on the cheek.* "I'll back in a minute!"

Jac rushed into Em's office.

"Good! I need to talk to you, Jac! You came back yesterday! What happened to Brooks ? Rumors are flying, most of them sound crazy! How did Brooks cut his arm? There's a new lock on his door and I don't have a key. What do you think is happening?"

Jac closed and locked the door. "I don't want anyone else to hear what I have to tell you! As for the new lock, I'd give anything to know who changed it. Brooks is still in the hospital and won't be going anywhere for a few more days! Janice and I came here yesterday afternoon, no one was here. I had just shown her around when we heard the sound of a drill. Or, what sounded like a drill. It just didn't make sense to us. Who'd be using a drill, and on a Sunday to boot! Since we didn't know 'who' or 'what,' we were *slowly* walking toward the noise when Brook's door opened and he literally fell into our arms! Janice was amazing! She stopped the blood. Em, here's the interesting thing! You won't believe it, but as soon as the firemen had Brooks stabilized he 'strongly' cautioned us to stay out of his room. Of course, that was the first thing we did! You had to see it! He had been drilling a hole into the floor by his desk. It allowed him to watch what looked like people working on the floor below. I thought the first floor only consisted of a Reception area! Did you know about the floor below? The new hole was just clean enough so we could see some cubicles and strange people below!"

Janice knocked quietly; Jac opened the door. "I just told Em about the hole and the room downstairs."

Em protested. "You're crazy, there's nothing below this floor! I can prove it! All I have to do is measure inside and outside of the Reception area!" *Em could not, would not believe it!*

"I wish you would prove us wrong!"

"I consider you a rational individual, but I think, this time, you're off your rocker! The three of us should go outside into the fresh air. The less time I spend in this rat-hole the better I feel!"

"Suits me!"

"Five dollars I'm right!"

"I'm usually not a betting-man, but I'm on it– this time, Em, my new-found, financial benefactor!"

"Now I remember why I hate attorneys!" *Em continued to smile as they all took part in measuring the front of the building. They knew the inside Reception draperies extended wall-to-wall, which allowed an accurate measure.*

14. A Matter Of Trust

"GOD DAMN, GO TO HELL! Sorry, I'm not a man to swear very often! But you WIN! The Reception area IS... fifteen feet narrower than the end cornice! What the hell is happening in that extra, fifteen feet?"

"Personally, I don't have a clue. Privately, I wouldn't want anyone to know how intrigued I am. I have to smile when I think of what you told me about 'nefarious goings on' in the office. Seems to me we must relegate everything to a 'wait-see' file until we solve this one. I know, 'solve' is a poor choice of words. I'm no Joe Friday! But, I would like to get all the facts! Seems to me, we should do whatever is legal. One, either get into Brook's room or, two, find the entrance to the other second floor. Or, do you or Janice have a better plan?"

"I'm with you, Jac. I don't have clue! Just a bunch of questions! Do you suppose Brooks has been using the operation for something other than insurance?"

"I'd say, Positively! It has to be, otherwise, why the secrecy?"

"If you fellows don't mind my saying, I think Jac has the best idea. If Brooks really has employees down there, then there has to be more than one door in and out. Em, do you have any idea of how we can get a hold of the building's plans? You could say there's a need to check some fire policy…or other."

"Terrific idea! Now you see why I wanted her by my side!" *Jac gave her a quick, one-arm hug.*

"Okay, I'll start making calls now. In the meantime, how about taking this stack of files off my desk! Don't tell me 'thank you' I'm just glad to get rid of them. Don't forget I promised to give you the ones we usu-ally 'send-out' to other attorneys, Good luck in starting that private practice. Let me know what the two of you need." *Em was relieved to have the new man on his side and he intended to do everything in his power to keep him happy!*

It took the both of them to carry the files back to Jac's office. "Well, dear friend, we have our work cut-out for us! Do you still want that wall between Us? My thought is we can wait until clients begin to arrive. In the meantime, I can either get a 'drink' at the water cooler, listening as I drink, or, I can go into Em's room to wait. I'm sure he won't mind."

"Great! The first thing we do is make each case part of a file that contains pertinent information. I can make up a template for you! *Her kiss on his cheek was the best yet; warm and comfortable! Jac was learning.*

"I'm up to 129, how's that for a start, Mr. Attorney?"

"All you'd have to do is check the size of my smile! Sounds like heavenly, music to my ears…that's how it is!"

The phone rang. "Yes, it's me, Mr. Brooks, how are you doing? We were.." Brooks cut Jac off. "Shut up and listen. I don't know how much longer I'm going to have to be in this place! I don't even know what's wrong with me." *Jac was thinking he knew what was wrong. The poor fool nearly bled to death!* Brooks was going on about 'private business being private business' and confidentiality had to be 'kept' no matter what was said. On, and on, for the better part twenty-minutes. Jac interrupted him.

"Mr. Brooks, you know I can be trusted. After what I saw yesterday, I think I have a much better relationship with 'honesty' than you do! As for 'confidentially,' it rarely is a two-way street. I am a State licensed attorney, and yes, I will always keep your confidentiality if and when you are my client." *Jac heard a loud spasm of coughing! He was told to hang-up! Mr. Brooks was in 'need of emergency attention.'*

Jac dialed Em's number, "Em, tell me, who signs the paychecks?"

15. The Room Downstairs

Jac picked up Janice an hour early. "Em thinks he has the right tool that will allow entrance to Brook's office. He's leaving it in my office so we can start investigating before he gets in this morning. Seems his wife is on a tear about something or other."

"Any news about, Brooks?"

"Confidentiality dictates behavior in that hospital. Anyone wanting information has to be a member of his family, so the answer, is 'no!'"

Em had followed through on Jac's request. The awkward looking tool was leaning on a chair. Jac attempted to lift the heavy, steel cutter. "My God, the thing weighs a ton!"

"It's going to take both of us to work it. And, for a girl, I'm stronger than I look."

"Okay, I see what we need to do. I'll hold the bit as straight as I can against the lock while you turn it on. I wonder where Em got this contraption? It looks a little FBI'ish. I wonder if it's legal?"

"No questions, just work! And, remember we agreed... no questions of any kind!" *Janice hoped Jac hadn't notice her involuntary flinch at the mention of the Bureau. Just another one of those things she would have to explain later.*

"No, I do NOT remember! I am asking again, is it le.." *Jac stumbled...in truth, was thrown forward as the door opened inward.*

Em caught up with the pair just as the door opened. "A great tool, right? Am I a genius, or what! That was not a question!"

"Granted, you have talents beyond all expectations, Em! Check the hole."

Em, crossed the floor. "What hole? I knew there was no hole!"

"What are you saying? I'm telling you, there is a hole! Move over, let me see."

"So where is it?" *Em sounded disappointed and disgusted.*

"Not so fast! What is this?" Jac had taken a nail file from a breast pocket and began scrapping away a fresh coat of paint and some nearly hardened cement. *He dismissed the odd look that crossed Janice's face.* "There, my friend is your hole!"

"I don't believe what I'm seeing! Damn, from what I can see, there must be twenty or twenty-five people down there. Have a look, do they look strange to you?" Em stumbled backward into the first available chair.

"Strange, how?"

"I'm not sure, it's just the shape of their heads and shoulders."

Jac started to laugh, "Aliens from another planet?"

"Hey, stop it! I'm serious. Could they be Japanese?"

"I wouldn't say that was very likely! We just finished a war! And, I'm NOT going back!"

"I'm just saying, take another look for yourself!"

Janice interrupted, "Mind if I take a peek?"

"Help yourself."

Jac, I see what he means; MY God, they *are* Japanese!"

"You've got to be kidding! Let me see!" *Jac couldn't believe it! Those men were Japanese. He couldn't begin to fathom why they were there or what they could possibly be doing!*

"We better get out of here, I think I just heard Jinksey! What an inopportune time *for him to make an appearance!" Em replaced Brook's desk chair.*

"I wanted to meet him, but not at this moment. Is it agreed that we tell him nothing about the room or the workers?"

"That sounds like the smart thing to do as far as I'm concerned, Jac!"

"Good! Let's make a casual retreat."

Jac and Janice had hardly gotten themselves seated when a rather short, sun-bronze, well- developed body, sprinted into the office.

"Boy, stay away a couple of days and just look what happens! Most of it great! *His eyes had made a thorough examination north and south, east and west of Janice's silhouette.* And, shall I guess who you are? Let's see, old 'Brooksie' finally got wise to Em and you are the replacement! Did I guess right?"

Janice surprised Jac by saying, in a rather stern voice, "NOT by a mile!" *Janice could only think, "….What a CREEP!*

"Happy to finally meet you, I'm Jac Cartwright, the new in-house attorney."

Jinksey's tan gave-way to a pale shade of grey.

"Not feeling well, Janice asked?"

Jac explained the new arrangement within the office and introduced Janice as his secretary. He thought Jinsksey took the news rather well considering he hadn't expected anyone to be there. He would, no doubt, want to check the insurance applications as soon as possible. Jac had explained the situation to Janice yesterday so she was fully aware of his criminal activity.

"Since you've been away, Mr. Jinksey, is there anything I can help you with?"

Jac had to smile to himself, Janice's timing was PERFECT! Poor Jinksey seemed to be a bit greyer.

"I don't need any help! And, the name is Jankowski" *The office door slammed as Jinksey made a hasty retreat.* "OH, MY GOD! Oh, my god! I CAN'T STAND THE PAIN! I NEED HELP! SOMEBODY HELP!

Everyone ran to Jinksey's office. He was holding his right arm and swaying back and forth as though it lessened the pain.

"What the hell did you do? You were only here a minute!"

"Nothing! Oh. GOD, THE PAIN! I think it's broken! I hurt it on a backhand this morning, but I didn't think … JUST GET ME AN AMBULANCE!"

Just like Brooks, Jinksey had a last minute assignment, this one for Em, "Don't let anyone touch the new 'apps,' I'll take care of them tomorrow!" Em knew full-well what he meant!

The remainder of the day was uneventful by comparison.

"Oh, by the way, Jac, I wanted to tell you that the high school seniors who volunteer each Monday will be coming tomorrow. If you need any extra help just let me know."

16. Getting Settled

"I want to stop at the Western Union before we eat. My money should have arrived today. Any telegram would have been sent to the apartment."

"Sounds good, Jac. I think there's a Bar and Grill near Western Union, if I remember correctly. I'll bet you've never eaten in a Bar and Grill. Right?"

"You got it! Sounds interesting though. What kind of food; sandwiches and beer?"

"Great steaks, seafood, whatever, it's a good variety. I like their T-Bones. Costs ninety-five cents, but they give you everything, including a drink and dessert."

Jac was in and out of the office within five minutes. The smile on his face told Janice 'all must be right with the money Gods'.

"Didn't take you very long!"

"Got my money, I only asked for two-thousand dollars, mom sent four. Guess I can handle that."

"A little extra never hurts."

"I know, but I don't really need it with my new job. I'll just put it into a bank and forget about it for a while."

"I have a suggestion, tell you about it when we get inside."

They parked and walked to the front door of Casey's Gentle Bar and Grill. Janice told Jac the sign used to say Casey's Gentlemen's Bar and Grill, when Casey's wife saw it, the story goes, she blew her stack and made him change it immediately.

The Grill lived up to Janice's review.

"Boy, you were right, this steak is wonderful!"

"To change the subject, what did you think about the scene this afternoon. I mean, I couldn't tell if your Mr. Jinksey was more worried about his arm, or terrified to leave the office. I really thought he looked *terrified*. What was your assessment?"

"I'm not the one to ask. I had never met him before. I think it very well may have been a combination of pain and fear. Since this is the time of the month Em said Jinksey did his 'dance around the incoming monies' I would say there's a good possibility he's not resting too well right now. We should know something by tomorrow."

"Well, I have to admit I'm more curious about that room below us."

"I'm with you! I can't even begin to hazard a guess. Whatever it is, I'm not too sure I should be a part of it, but I'm willing to learn more about the activity going on down there!"

"Not to change the subject, have you ever tasted better pie?"

"Oh, Please! Don't talk to me about 'pie.'" Jac told her about the Galley Cook and his 'too flakey' lemon pie. Janice couldn't stop laughing.

"If you don't mind, I didn't think it was that funny! Anyway, I now know… pie isn't supposed to be chewy."

"I wasn't laughing 'at' you, just with 'you,' I would have loved to have seen his face when you said it wasn't 'chewy' enough!"

"Well, I only wish everything was as easy to solve as pie-making! We should learn more from Em tomorrow. How about tonight? I'm not trying to rush things, but I think we should have plans laid out. What do you think?"

Janice was glad Jac couldn't read her mind. Jac's behavior had been nothing related to 'rushing it.' She had to admit a lot had happened within a couple of days. Things that other men she had known would have taken advantage of…long before now! "I'm not comfortable going to your apartment. I'm afraid of your landlady. She acts like she owns you. And, my apartment is shared with my two roommates. So, I don't know what to tell you."

"Let's not worry about it now. We've both had a huge day and can use a good rest. I'll pick you up in the morning. Okay?"

Jac knew he had to find an appropriate apartment. The room was cramped and the Murphy was a foot too short. *Being six foot-four almost kept him from becoming a flyer.*

☙

17. End Of Perfect Employment

Jac and Janice were caught-up on office news as soon as they walked up the stairs… Jinksey was still in the hospital! His arm was broken in two places. He had had four surgeries last night. His tennis arm now sports two steel rods, and, he's not expected to return for a month.

Em called to them. "Come in, kids. Don't believe everything you hear. I'll bet Jinksey is back by the end of the week if he has to be carried. I was able to lock his bottom-drawer."

"What did you do about the new 'applications.'"

"Nothing! Do you think I'm nuts? I'm not about to go to jail for someone else…period!"

"Thanks! I was afraid you might be tempted, and I would lose a good friend, and possibly, my future investigator!"

෩

The remainder of the week was uneventful as far as the three friends were concerned. Jac and Janice spent every free moment scanning rental ads. Jac had to move! *His Landlady offered to reduce his rent if he would drive for her.* "I do so hate to deal with that tank of a thing." Jac told her she reminded him of Gloria Swanson.

Friday morning Janice informed Jac she had finished calling all of Jac's original contacts. Letting everyone know Jac now had an office and was ready to care for any legal work they might want to send his way.

"You called every one of them?"

"Everyone on the yellow pad."

"Bless you!"

"Well, do I rate anything special? Like a kiss, maybe?"

Jac blushed, "Come here, you rate a big one right on the cheek!"

"Sez, you! "Janice bent over…making her mouth available to the kiss."That's much better!"

"But somebody might see us!"

"I don't mind, and neither should you. We are the only sane people here."

"Janice, let's go to lunch. Em came by while you were getting a drink; he wants to meet us for lunch. He said he's paying."

"Gosh, Jac, he must have really big news!

Jac was about to respond when they both heard a sudden commotion in the hallway.

"What the HELL ARE YOU DOING HERE, JINKS – IT'S ONLY FRIDAY? Everyone heard Em scream "You are going to ruin your arm… for GOOD!

How the hell did you get here? Better! What the hell do you want?"

"What the hell do you think I 'want!'" Jinksey could hardly speak. Pain medication or not, he was experiencing a gut-wrenching pain.

"I told you I would take care of things for you. And, I did! I locked everything up tight as a drum!" Em helped him into his office.

"Okay, fine. Just leave me alone. You can unlock and open the drawer before you leave."

"Good as done." *'You fool!' was added under Em's breath.*

Jac had just returned to his office when the phone rang. "Mr. Cartwright's office, how may we help you?" Janice was perfect! "One moment Mr. Croft, you say you are with the State and wish to speak with Mr. Cartwright, one moment, please." She handed the phone to Jac; her frown said there was something to worry about.

"This is Jac Cartwright, how may I help you?"

"You can't. I want to help you! I thought you were a nice kid when you visited Keen Transport. I was the only other man in a suit besides you in their office."

Jac broke-in, "I remember you. I heard much of what you were suggesting to help them, and thought at the time, you were a very caring person …especially, for a State Agent."

"Thanks for the good thoughts, however you need to know your Company is in big trouble! I know you don't have anything to do with the trouble, that's why

I'm warning you. Get out of there! NOW! The Company has been placed in the Hands of The State's Receivers. Don't be there when they get there. Call me at ORIAN 52364 tomorrow."

"What is it, Jac? You're as white as a sheet!"

"Don't say anything. Just do as I ask, I'll explain later! You get all the lists of clients, not the files, just leave them. Take anything personal. Don't leave anything behind! I've got to warn Em!" *How did Croft know I was going to work here?* Jac was too shocked to think much about anything other than following Croft's "suggestions."

"NO, SHIT!" Everyone in the building must have heard Em.

"What the hell are you yelling about?" Jinksey had called from his office. But he couldn't have been heard by very many. He was too weak!

The three friends exited the building just as a black limo pulled-up in front of the stairs.

"Em, wasn't that Brooks getting out of that car?"

"I think you're right, Jac. Should we tell him anything?"

"Hell, no! I think it's about him and the room downstairs. Why else would the State take over a Company like Whitehouse?"

"I guess you're right."

"Well, do we still want to eat?"

"Not me, Janice, I have to run to the bank and withdraw all my money! The State will freeze every employee's account!"

"That's terrible, Em, Good luck! Jac and I will be at Casey's Bar and Grill if you finish in time! Is that Okay with you, Jac? Sorry I didn't ask first. I guess I was just feeling so awful for Em ...I wasn't thinking."

"God, yes, it's fine. I just hadn't thought 'bank accounts' but, that is what municipalities do when they take over any entity. God, what a mess! So much for the 'perfect' job. But, I want you to promise not to worry. I'm lucky, I hadn't signed any employ-ment papers yet! I'm glad mom sent extra money, and there's more where that came from. I'll just rent an office and we will start-up with the clients on your list."

"Is that legal?"

"Of course it is! They still have a case against Whitehouse, we may have to wait for our money, but that's Okay! It will be a start. Are you with me?

"Yes."

Jac finally gave her, what she described as a 'boffo kiss,' *On the forehead.* "Better on the forehead than ...nothing." *Janice muttered something about 'when' under her breath.* Ignoring Jac's frown, Janice said, "Let's just have a light lunch, then I'll take you to the May Company so you can select some inexpen-sive furniture for the office you don't have yet."

"How far? And, where will we put the items?"

"At the corner of Wilshire and Ls Brea. And, in your new office!" She gave her skirt a twist and tossed winked in Jac's direction.

Oblivious to Janice's efforts to obtain some per-sonal attention, Jac had only one question, "Shouldn't we get an office, first?"

"Not a problem. *Janice was determined to do better next time,* "Don't ask me why, but I have been looking at ads for office rentals. I think I know where a perfect, low-cost, well situated office is located. It's at the corner of Fifth and Western. Just one block North of Wilshire. It's the Haas Building, third floor, and larger than your apartment. five-hundred square-feet. How does that sound?"

Jac didn't have the opportunity to answer. The Grill door opened.

"Hi, all! Made it to the bank. I'm not certain, but I think the State Men came into the bank just as I was leaving. Most of us banked at the California Bank. It was easy for us to take turns banking for each other on pay days. Oh, well, those were the days! Have you eaten yet?"

"Not yet."

"Good, I'm starved! Okay, what have I missed?"

"I'll bring you up to snuff after we eat. All you need to know is, the three of us are 'in business!'"

Em put down the menu, "We're...WHAT?

∽

18. New Set-Up

The Haas Building was perfect! The bathroom was next door to the suite, and the only other tenant on the second floor was a medical doctor. "Some kind of foreigner," according to Jac's assessment. "How come all the offices are closed today? And, where did the three chairs come from?"

"From the office of the building, so we can get by until we get our furniture. The Docs are all Jewish; Saturday is their Sabbath. There are a lot of Jewish doctors in Los Angeles! Do you have anything against Jews?"

"Of course, NOT! I just didn't recognize what he was, that's all."

"Boy, you guys, it's a good thing Brooks isn't here. He can't stand Jews! Can you believe it? Him hiring Jinksey and not knowing he was a Jew! We all had a good laugh on that one! I even asked him one day, what Jinksey was, he told me Jinkowski was Polish and probably Catholic. He never paid attention when Jinksey talked about attending "Temple." Boy, what an intellectual!"

Janice laughed. Jac wondered why, but said nothing.

"How about an office budget, we want to save every penny possible! What do you think?"

She 'hit' the right note! Saving money was the objective of every 'depression kid!' God, he was so glad Janice had happened along. He experienced a fleeting thought; he wondered if this was what 'love' felt like. He had the same feeling when his mom did something special; just for him. *That's when she would call him her Kitten Cat. Easy to understand why dad was called Nicas The Dog; short for Nicademus. Not a very loving guy!*

"About the budget. You haven't said a word, Em! How about setting up some books for us. We hereby dub thee, Sir, Emmery, The Great – Keeper of Goods! All kidding aside, we need you!"

"Don't laugh, I could cry! I can't tell you how special it feels to be needed, and most of all, trusted! Thanks."

"I second everything Jac said! We need you, Em. We will be the invincible three! What are we going to call us?"

"Legally, we better stick to Cartwright and Associates."

"We still have time to shop for some furniture."

"Do you think it would be better if we went to the Navy Exchange? They usually have the best bargains."

"Where is it?"

"I think the closest I could find is in Long Beach, where ever that is located."

"Do they deliver?"

"No. I guess you're right. Let's get to the chore of shopping. *Shaking his head.* I'd rather have a tooth pulled!"

"It's just a lack of a very important life experience. Right, Janice?"

Janice patted Em's back as she passed. "You bet! We'll get him into shape in the blink-of-an-eye at this rate. Do the two of you realize, twenty-four hours ago we were each thinking about the new alliance in which we were about engage? I can't believe it myself!"

The May Company's parking lot was full! "My God, Janice, does everyone shop on Saturday night?"

"The store stays open until nine o'clock and gives the working folks a chance have a night out. As for our office... the rooms are a little dark, how about getting some color in the sitting room. You will want clients to feel comfortable. Look at this rattan set. You get a two-cushion loveseat, two side-chairs, a four-foot corner table, and a coffee table! I love the Hawaiian print."

"How much does it cost?"

"The tag says, "... reduced to a hundred-twenty dollars from three-hundred fifty. Today Only."

"Do you think it's worth that much?"

"Jeese, Jac, grab it! My wife and I have never seen this much for so little!"

"Well, if the two of you think we should, then we will!"

Jac began to feel like a little kid on Christmas! Strange, but good! He hated the two-day wait for delivery!

"I hate to break this up! My wife will be 'nuts' by now; she usually calls Whitehouse every day. And, I'm more than late. Boy, wait till she hears everything! Can I get a lift back to my car?"

"Of, Course!"

They exited the store on the Wilshire side. The newsboy was calling:

"Whitehouse Insurance Company Cut-Down By Sixteen Year-Old!" He continued to repeat the head-line.

"Oh, My God!"

The three were too stunned to move!

Janice was the first to speak. "What do you think happened?"

They each bought a paper. And, agreed to meet across the street from the new office for breakfast at seven o'clock in the morning.

19. After The Storm

The simple two-egg breakfast was nearly finished before anyone spoke of any substantive issue. And there were a plethora of issues available.

"Okay, I gave this a lot of thought and I think the paper had it all wrong. They said the Owner was taking illegal money from the Company. Not true! Brooks was doing *something,* but it wasn't taking 'money from the 'til.' Remember the room downstairs, it looked like much bigger fish he was after! I was trying to think back to last Tuesday and yesterday morning. The school volunteer came into my office Tuesday and wanted to know what to do with the papers she had in her hands. I didn't think to ask what they were; I just said, "You've been here long enough to use you own resourcefulness. I, regrettably, think she did. I can only think that she had a batch of punch cards, not the files from Jinksey's office, that accumulated every so often in the Outbound Tray. She probably ran them through the machine and sent the information to the State by 'telephonic' messenger! A huge red flag must have go off in more than one office! Four years difference in supposedly, collected fees, on insurance never registered with the State! I can only imagine what happened next! Boy, you were lucky not to be involved. The stigma of association with a State Insurance Take-Over wouldn't do much for your vita."

"Amen! But! Guys! Doesn't it sound like they don't know anything about Brook's 'downstairs' business!'" Janice continued to speak, "My, God. What about those people?"

"By, God, You're right! I don't know about the two of you but "I love a mystery" to steal a title from what was my favorite radio show. I think I'm going to find the outside door that HAS to be there! And, by the way, my wife wanted to come today. She said she didn't believe what I am doing. She thinks I'm gambling or some damn fool thing!"

Jac offered, "Maybe she can help. But before we go off half-cocked, we need to take care of some important office decisions." The three of them spent a hour, squatted on the floor since there were no tables, writing individual suggestions, schedules and lists of personal 'wants' on yellow pads.

"We can't do anything without communication with the outside world! So, I'm bent on getting us three phones. I have a good idea about some desks. Downtown, skid-row area has some used office furniture stores for cheap and they deliver. Jac and I can go as soon as I'm able to get our phone appointment."

"I'm sure glad you're here, Janice! Em and I are depending on your good sense for a great beginning! Right, Em?"

"You, bet! Where did you say you found this, gem?"

"Never mind, fella! Let's just get with it!"

Janice left ample time for desk shopping. Everyone remained open on Sunday. Jac spent his time formulating some 'introduction letters' for the men he had contacted when he had searched for a job. He also made a list of the information needed to legitimize Em as an investigator.

Then there were the many licenses; a business license for the office, a license for Em, and some insurance against a 'slip and fall' in the office. He wasn't sure if California required special banking practices when holding money 'for another?' *Janice came to mind, again, for the umpteenth time!*

Em began to gather his notes, "Jac, I need to get home before my wife has a hissy!"

෴

The shopping excursions and office planning left both very tired. Jac and Janice were glad to take time out to eat. Jac was introduced to Philippe's, downtown, near China town, off Hill Street. The Beef Dip Sandwich was reported to be world renowned! As far as Jac was concerned, the reputation was "dead-on!" Sawdust floor and all! He had never seen anything like this place. *Los Angeles was just one surprise after another!*

"I don't know about you, but I would like to see at least one of the apartments you have on your list. If

I have to stay one more night in my black bathroom I won't be responsible for my actions!"

"It can't be that bad! You've had to put-up with worse, Jac and you know it!" Janice gave a small laugh with a huge grin, "Or, do you really miss me?"

"You know the answer to that!"

"Boy, never let it be said 'you sweep women off their feet!"

"I don't know what you are talking about."

"I guess that's what makes you rather special."

"Shall we leave before it gets dark?"

৶

20. Second Apartment

"How are you enjoying the sightseeing? The only reason I wanted to drive was so that you would have an opportunity to become more acquainted with your new neighborhood. I deliberately started at the beginning of Wilshire Boulevard so you could see all the old buildings. Many professionals rent in the area. But, people are saying 'go west of Western' for the more prestigious firms. At least that's what I've heard."

"Well, I have news for you, Lady. I wasn't kidding when I said I walked the entire north side of Wilshire, from where it starts to where I found Whitehouse Insurance!"

"My, God, no wonder you have so many names and numbers on your yellow pad! You are nothing short of a wonder, Jac! Were I not driving, I'd give you a big kiss!"

Jac smiled broadly, "Is that all you think about?"

"Do you mind?"

"Not at all!"

It was getting dark when Janice pulled-up in front of a three story apartment. Just south of Olympic and half-a-block west of Western.

"This is one of the Grand Old Ladies of the thirties. The ad sounds great. It is more money, though."

"Well, let's give it a look."

The two of them returned from the building laughing and smiling like a couple of kids! Jac was giving Janice's shoulder a squeeze from time to time as though to punctuate his happiness.

"I can't believe it! The same money! The same services offered! I don't have to buy a thing. Two bedrooms, a kitchen with room for two, a sitting room, a balcony! I can even walk to work if I want. My, God, wait till my mother sees it!"

"Your Mother? Will she be coming soon?"

Jac heard the catch in Janice's voice.

"Not till winter."

"This winter?"

"Next winter, maybe." Jac smiled to himself. "Mom usually helps me when I move to a new apartment. She was wonderful to spend so much time with me when I was in law school. I guess she doesn't mind being away from dad!"

"I think I know what you are thinking!" *Janice hoped Jac didn't get the wrong impression of her response about a woman Janice already knew. She reminded herself to be more careful!* "You want to call Em and have the two of them join us for a second celebration. Right?"

"Not even close! This is our celebration! This time I want to go somewhere really fancy!"

"I know just the place!" Janice started her car.

"On Wilshire?"

"You got it, Jac! Everything of any singular value is on Wilshire Boulevard! And, here we are! This is the one and only Ambassador Hotel!" Janice gave her keys to the parking attendant.

"Let's walk around to the front of the building, I want you to get the full effect! Wilshire Boulevard is magic at night."

"What's that place across the street? It looks like a hat!" Jac winced a bit, "Only in Los Angeles!"

"We'll go there for lunch sometime. You will love the food and the atmosphere! It's called the Brown Derby. Do you like it?"

"I think I have much to become acquainted with in this city! But, yes, I like it!"

The meal at the Ambassador Hotel awakened a renewed fire within Jac! He reaffirmed his pledge to 'make the courtroom on his first try!' He was determined to make money available for meals like this, and any other luxury that pleased his fancy! "Do you have any inkling of what I was feeling as we ate? I mean, this, all of this is what I want! I want the where-with-all to eat where ever I want! I want everyone to know that 'river kids' can make good in a big city! I'm so full of feeling I could kiss you right out here in front of everybody! "Jac paused. "I'm just so happy I could cry!"

Janice was too surprised at Jac's 'awakening' to speak. She took his hand and pressed it tightly into hers. The two stood quietly, in the cool night air, watching traffic.

"How would you like to spend the night with me? Everything looked clean enough, wouldn't you say?""

"How about if we get your things from the Witch, first?"

"If you are not too tired, that suits me fine."

"Jac, we need to have a straight talk about living arrangements. I'm never quite sure which page you're on. You are too important to me to have some silly misunderstanding spoil things."

"I'm sorry I wasn't trying to take advantage! And, I agree with you! We will have a talk. But, not tonight, we both need our sleep."

21. It's In The Bank

"Hey, Guys, this seven a.m. breakfast could become a habit! How about we go Dutch treat?"

"Not until you are getting a paycheck from me! That's final! What will you need to get your Investigator's license.?"

"Not to worry. It's in the works. I should have it by the end of the month."

"Good. We can go over some of the contacts Janice has arranged and make our plans accordingly."

"Jac, I have the letters ready for the two of you to go over and edit."

"Oh, yes. And, I Super Investigator To Be, have a budget set-out for the next six months. Knowing you, Jac, it probably won't take you six month to get started."

"I hope not. By the way, how about showing me where California Bank is located and I can start an account. I think I'll have my mom send all my money. And, the three of us can check on that 'outside door' you wanted to find, Em."

"Sounds good."

Banking was new to Jac. During the War, he needed only send money home and mom would invest it in Postal Notes. It was a wonderful way to save. However, post-War banking was another entity unto its self. There were several kinds of accounts. Some were interest bearing, some not; others were strictly for saving with penalty on with-drawl before certain dates. The bank manager suggested three different accounts to begin Jac's business. One would be for his personal use. But it required he have some-one as a beneficiary. *He thought about listing mom, then he thought of Janice.* A second account would serve the office, including all employee deductions as well as salary, and equipment. *Jac gave a little chuckle when he thought of establishing a petty-cash account. Poor, Em. Jac, hoped he wouldn't be put-ting temptation in Em's way!* A third account would be needed for each client. *Jac had never heard of this law. Of course, Los Angeles was different!* Simply stated, all monies to be kept separate and distinct, one from another! No co-mingling!

Jac and Janice had to sign 'office account' papers; Janice had the beneficiary card to sign (the look on her face showed how over-come she was by the trust Jac was placing in her), and Em signed for the office account.

"Jac, I don't have the words right now to tell you how much I appreciate the trust you placed in me, I will never let you down!" With a light tap on Jac's arm, Em added, "Even with the petty cash." That got a laugh out of all three of them.

∽

22. We Love A Mystry

"What if I park here. Is this close enough?"

"Suits me, Janice. One short block to the Insurance building isn't much of a walk, besides with all the great food I've been blessed with over the past few days I really need to walk!"

"In a pig's eye! Jac you look fine to these eyes!"

"Ditto, me too. Janice and I see alike!"

"Thanks to both of you."

"I don't know about the two of you, but I could NOT see any area that could be any kind of façade for anything akin to an opening."

"Okay, they have to have a way to get in and out! Now, where do we start. We can't go into Whitehouse Insurance. How about checking the building behind for a bridge or something that allows egress?"

"Good thinking!"

"Janice you're a woman."

"Gee, thanks, Fella!"

"NO! What I mean is, if we want to check a different building or doorway, it's not likely anyone would get upset if it was a woman and not just some man snooping!"

"Sorry. Gottch'a. And, I do agree."

In horrible pitch, Em begins singing, "Gee, ain't it great to have a Gal around the …"

Jac interrupted, "I agree, let's go around to the front of the building that opens on the back street. Hey! Look! There's hardly ANY space between the buildings! I knew it! They have to be entering from THIS building…not Whitehouse! This get better all the time!"

"Okay, Guys, I'll go in and see what kind of operation they have. It may be that there are offices, and who knows, there may have one for rent! That would give all of us an excuse to go in and look around!"

"Great idea! Looks like Em agrees too."

The lobby was dark, just one small light at the top of a very high ceiling. This must have been a very grand building at another time, It still had great 'bones' as Jac had once heard an architect say. There were no signs, no mail boxes, no lighted transoms, only doors and an elevator.

"No harm, or foul! At least, that's what we believed in the Navy! Let's see where this elevator takes us."

"Jac, we don't know what we might get into, and who we might get 'into it with,' so let's think before we jump!"

"Goes for me too!" Both men were in agreement.

"Okay, we are only interested in a space somewhere between what was our main floor and our second floor. Right? Okay, since we don't have a tape measure with us.."

Em interrupted, "At least not this time."

"Right! We start on the second floor and check for a mezzanine, alright?"

Em offered, "Looks just like our second floor, at least for the hallway, since it's the only area we can see."

True, at first glance. What else do you notice?"

"Jac, I know. Look, Em all the room numbers start with the number "three!"

"So, that means there's a number "two" floor or a mezzanine ..... somewhere."

"Right! Let's find it!"

"Janice, while Em and I stand at the end of the hall, you start knocking on some doors and see if you get anyone's attention. Just play it by ear."

Janice started at the far end of the hall. No answer until she had almost completed the assignment, three doors down from where the men were standing.

"Hello. I was hoping I could be directed to the building manager, or the Office of The Building."

"No speakee!" The door slammed shut!

"If at first.." Janice smiled as she approached the next door. She knocked smartly! No answer. The last door was opened by a nice looking, young man in his twenties, dressed in a three-pieced suit.

"May I help you?" *The breadth of his grin said, "I hope so!"*

"I'm looking for the building manager, I'll wager you can help me."

"I'm afraid not, I'm just visiting my uncle. Perhaps he can help you." He turned, and as he walked into

117

the room, Janice was able to view a familiar tableaux; both males and females worked, heads bent, at what appeared to be small, green, very modern typewriters. The machines were almost soundless! Not at all like Jac's Royal. *The clickity-clack of a Royal could always be heard in more than in just 'a next-room.* The three cohorts stood motionless for several seconds. The return of the young man, obviously, Oriental, brought them back to the present situation with a bit of a jolt! Not one of the three volunteered to take command of the situation.

The young man had returned to say, "My uncle says he has rented all of the available space at this address, but he suggests you contact a Mr. Brooks at Whitehouse Insurance, just around the corner. He might know of other properties that are available."

Again, silence from the 'mighty three.' Finally, Em broke the silence with, "Those are the quietest type-writers I have ever heard! Where do they come from?"

"I'm not sure, I'll ask my uncle. The young man disappeared for a second or two then returned with, "My uncle says they are from either Italy or France. He's not quite certain. I did copy the name for you. I thought you seemed quite interested."

The three almost bowed as they said their 'Thank You's and 'Goodbye's,' while slowly backing away from the open door.

They were a half-block away before they slowed their pace. All three began laughing!

"Aren't we the great investigators?" Janice could hardly contain herself.

"Speak for yourself, I did not hear, even a gasp from the two of you. I had to do all the talking! Thanks a heap, Gang!"

"My God, Em, You were wonderful. The way you were able to come up with that question about the typewriter. I would never in a thousand years have thought to ask a completely, neutral question. No suspicions could possibly have been aroused! Boy, did I pick a winner when I found you! I can't tell you how convinced I am that we will be an unbeatable team!"

"Love those words of praise; however I believe I will garner a few more of those words when I tell you what I did! I'll bet the two of you didn't notice how carefully I took the scrap of paper. How I gently slipped it into my pocket, being careful to only touch an outer edge."

Janice interrupted, "You old bloodhound! You plan to have the fingerprints checked, and maybe, identify the man while you are at it, RIGHT?"

"Correct! And, I know just the FBI man to do it for us!"

"Em, as your new Boss Man I'm giving you a raise!"

"How much, Boss? Another zero on my zero check?" Everyone chuckled.

"Call it women's curiosity, but I want to know what the note said."

"Me too, Em."

"It doesn't make much sense, it says only two words. The first is printed and says 'Olivetti.' I guess that's the name of the machine. The second is in cursive and only says 'stop.' What do the two of you make of it? For myself, I don't have a clue! I do think that if 'stop' had been printed it might have been part of some previous message and the name could be the one in cursive. Beats the heck out of me!"

"I'm with you. Got any suggestions, Janice?"

"Well, I don/t think there's much we can learn until we make a few plans, contact a few persons that might help and above all, remember we are three unemployed *Her mind had been spinning! The last thing she wanted to do was get involved in some nefarious goings-on! The Supervisor would be furious. No extra-curricular involvement!*

Jac surprised himself and everyone else! The kiss was long, hard and on the lips! "Now, so there won't be any question, I am never going to let this lady get away from me! Not in a million years! I need her!"

Janice was thrilled to hear the words, but an after-thought lingered a little too long. Was Jac all 'need' and no 'love' or at least some semblance of 'care?' She shook her head to clear away her thoughts and focus on the issues at hand.

"Okay, Fellas, what do I always suggest?"

The men answered in unison, "Let's go out and get something to eat!"

"Right, and I know just the place! As usual. It's at Olympic and Western, just a very small family Bar with home cooking, called O'Kelly's. A small menu, but everything is fresh and delicious."

"Sounds terrific, wish I could eat with you, duty calls. My wife will be waiting."

"Have you told her about your new job yet?"

"I haven't had the courage. I will soon."

"Why don't you pick her up and bring her along and the three of us can convince her of you great, new opportunity to become a respected member of society? License and all!"

"You know, that's a great idea! Meet you there in forty-five minutes." Janice and Jac ordered a glass of wine while they waited for Em. It was their first opportunity to relax. *Wonderful smells wafted through the small room, reminding Jac of Grandma Diffy. She was the only one able to cook more than tea and toast in his family. Her Irish dishes were the talk of the small town. Occasionally, she was asked to teach new brides, something that was overlooked when Jac's mom came along. Or, did she just refuse to learn. Knowing Granny, Jac thought the latter was more likely the truth.* Jac's reverie was interrupted!

"Here we are!"

Some twenty minutes passed before the usual pleasantries were finished, and with great result! Em's wife was glad to hear her husband, 'the poor blind dummy' would actually be bettering himself before he 'died.' She was less than gracious as she complained about anything and everything poor Em had ever done. Fortunately, the Special of the Day arrived, and everyone was hungry. Talk-time can be limited if one keeps one's mouth full! It worked like magic, up to and including the last cup of coffee and a second piece of peach cobbler.

"Em tells me you folks have a mystery on your hands. I love a mystery! Is there anything I can do to help?"

Em, waggles his finger in rapid succession behind his wife's back, indicating a strong 'NO.'

"Well," Jac begins with a broad smile," while we have very small quarters, do you think you would be interested in doing some over-flow typing for us at home. I could provide the typewriter?"

Em's wife beamed! "I would love to work on a mystery, or whatever! Let me at it!"

No one could say this woman lacked enthusiasm. She was ready. Jac had to believe it might even improve Em's home situation.

23. Now What

Jac's office was taking shape! So much had been accomplished in three days. The phones were in and working, the draperies hung, the used office furniture sporting a fresh coat of wax, inexpensive carpets covering old stains, waiting room furniture in place, and the three friends striking a comic pose of readiness at their own desks.

"Hey Fellas, do you think we look ready to take the town by storm?"

Em, countered, "Janice, I think we would have more business if you went down stairs and just stood near the front door!"

"Shame on both of you!" Jac was beaming from ear to ear. His team was really coming together. "I think we had better get to our list of Whitehouse clients if the two of you ever want to get paid" The telephone interrupt his next thought.

"Cartwright and Associates, how may I direct your call?" A short pause, "Jac, it's that State Man again! I hope we aren't in any trouble."

"Agent Croft, I didn't expect to be hearing from you so soon. We just this minute got settled into our new billet."

"It's a surprise to me too, Jac! I need to meet with you – Now! I don't mean to be difficult, but I have a very serious matter to discuss with you. Do you have a secretary yet?"

"Better than that! I also have a nearly, legal, Legal Investigator! His license is in the mail!"

"Do you trust them? Are you willing to vouch for them as good citizens of our Country?"

"Whoa! Of course, the answer is "yes," but you are going into some unfamiliar ground as far as I'm concerned! I learned, early on, not to volunteer for anything unless I know all of the 'ins and outs!'"

"I don't blame you Jac. It's just that I have very little time to put our plan into action. Will you please allow me to meet with you and your staff? I can be in your office in ten minutes!"

"Okay, the addre..."

Agent Croft interrupted, "I know where your new office is. See you!"

"Well, how do you like that? He said he knew where our new office is. I wish I knew what is happening."

Em volunteered, "It probably has to do with Jinksey and his defrauding the Company."

"I doubt it, Em. He want to speak to the three of us."

Janice gave a short gasp, "You mean me, too?"

"That's what he said."

There was a light knock on the inner-office door.

"Jeez, did either of you hear the hall door open?" Poor Em was white as the proverbial sheet.

"Glad you could find your way, or have you been here before?" Jac gave Agent Croft a weak smile and lead him to the chair next to his desk. "What the hell, is going on?"

Agent Croft, set his briefcase on the floor and removed his coat. "I have much to tell you – all three of you! So much has happened since I spoke with you last. I'm no longer with the state of California. This Whitehouse insurance thing is much larger than any of us ever believed possible. I am now on perma-nent loan to the FBI. You probably want to know what that has to do with you. If you will just hear me out I believe that you will be very willing to help. The day after we closed down the place we found some very interesting mail addressed to the president, Mr. Brooks.

Jac interrupted, "I thought this was about Mr. Jankowski!"

"Well, it was to begin with. Much of this mail we found was very damaging to the reputation of almost everyone working there, including you Mr. Emmery." Croft looked directly into Em's eyes. "It's a good thing Jac is your friend or you would be like the rest of the employees still under suspicion and being investi-gated."

"Thank you very much sir."

Jac could almost see Em's knees Shaking.

"Jac I want you to read this letter. It's only one of the several we found. We think this was one of the first written." Croft had Jac a wrinkled, partially torn letter written on very expensive, Japanese paper.

125

"When we finally get to our office I'll ask that you add your opinion to the report we will ask you to provide."

December 24, 1947
Tokyo Tsushin Kogyo K.K.
Tokyo, Japan
Most Honorable Jason Alfred Brooks:
We are most happy that your company's business is flourishing. We have many opportunities to maintain good record on you. You have now become one major large man in insurance industry. He is not always be in insurance. We know you from 1945 when you change big business. No more milling machine factory. No more war money. We know you have many buildings for sell or lease.

We like very much what you are now doing. You make very good business every day. We see you keep large account and local bank with change of name. We do not wish to bring harm to your family. We have only one design. We very much want you for friend and partner in new business. We help you. You get credit. We send you much new business. Business not aware to local authorities. We send you three helper to make change to your insurance building. After change we become partners. We pay you. You send money to Japan Bank. We be good, happy partners. Not safe to discuss our plan for you. You make good business. We both make money.

Name of new business is transistors. We know, you never heard of same before. Very new. School friend has information from friend, Akio Morita, who is friend of Masaru Ibuka who makes tape recorder. Tape recorder not very important. Only information about work in company called Bell laboratories. The need to learn connection. Big news. New transistors. I'll expect miracles from small object. Only Japanese workers have our big concern. We are sending to you 50 very good Japanese workers. You will be very surprised. They are not like normal workers. Many friends have many eyes and ears in your New Jersey. Bell laboratories will make us very rich. You too. No one must see Japanese workers. You will learn more later. We know you do not disappoint. We know you like money. You keep us happy. We keep you happy.

We dedicate to make good product to make happy all people and money for self. I will be in contact for future business.
With most sincere gratitude, I am,
Hoysu Toyma
Tokyo, Japan

Jac handed the letter back to Croft. "The gist of it sounds crazy, but it makes sense, believe it or not! However, I want to tell you I don't believe anyone of Japanese decent wrote that letter. I served with many Japanese Americans in the war, none spoke 'Pigeon-English!' I think it was meant to lure Brooks into something illegal! Like industrial sabotage. I guess the three of us have something to tell you about what we have been doing in our spare time" Jac glanced from Janice to Em, back to Croft, "I think we might just have the information for you, Agent Croft."

Croft carefully put the letter back into his briefcase, "Sounds like I should let you tell me your news before a say another word."

"Well, actually, there are four of us working on our puzzle, which by the way, happens to deal with your letter, the addressee, and the 'not normal' people mentioned in the letter."

Jac smiled and began to tell Croft about the 'second floor that wasn't there,' and the second building with more Japanese mechanical-type workers bend over typewriters. He told Croft about Brook's injury when he tried to cut a larger hole in his office floor; nearly cutting his arm off."

Croft never moved a muscle, he just sat…mouth agape. Croft interrupted, "Sorry team, I'm not cleared to listen to anything more on this subject. Just get your things and I'll get us a ride to the Bureau Office in Los Angeles. This is too big for a person as new to the Agency as myself." When he had recovered from initial shock Croft countered, "I might as well tell you why I'm here." He laid out the details of the Bureau's objectives for the three; great citizens, each with special talents, and the Bureau's need for information. "Your employment will be temporary, and we don't expect you will encounter danger of any kind. I'm prepared to offer $5000 as starter money for your office and a monthly salary of $350 a month for each of you.

Em was the first to speak, "Count me in!"

Janice nodded in agreement.

"What about you, Counselor, can we count on your services? You know, this would be a great thing to add to your vita. I knew the day I met you, you were a very special young man! Please, don't disappoint me; say yes."

"I don't mean to sound hesitant, I'm just not one to make snap-judgments or snap decisions. I always seem to need a little time to mull things over. As I think about it, working for the FBI would be a little like being in the military, only, this time, I would have an office and a couple special people to worry about. The other side of the coin says I would be of some help to my Government. I think I can handle your proposition. Would there be any time for me to work on my legal career?"

"Jac, it might just be the beginning of something very special. I expect you will be named Temporary Council for the Prosecution – a real coup for you!"

"Count me 'in'…I guess." A moment's hesitation, then, "Okay, whatever you say; when do we start?"

"I'll have the three of you picked up in an hour."

24. In The FBI

During the thirty-minute limousine ride, Croft explained his mission. "The government wants the three of you to assist in clearing up some very interesting 'puzzles' as you call them, regarding the true function of Whitehouse Insurance."

Em couldn't stifle his stage cough, "Which one of the five "functions" were you referring to, Mr. Croft?"

Jac interrupted, "Well, actually, there are four of us working on our puzzle, which by the way, happens to deal with: your letter, the addressee, and the 'not normal' people mentioned in the letter."

"I wish I knew which functions, I've only been with the bureau forty-eight hours." Croft pulled three fat envelopes from his case, "I need to get you all registered before we get there. You mentioned a fourth person, who is that?"

Jac, answered, "Oh, that's Em's wife who wants to do over-flow typing. And, by the way, what exactly do you mean when you say 'register us?'

Janice smiled, "Well, it will be one way we earn some money."

"Jac, we expect that you will continue to keep regular office hours and function like business as usual. We can't afford to let any of this become public knowledge…not yet!"

"So, if I understand what you just said, the three or four of u…"

Em interrupted, "Not my wife, please. Let's keep it to the three of us. I can keep her busy typing stuff for the Law office."

"Good thinking, Mr. Gant. And please forgive me, I believe I referred to you as just 'Em' before. That was very disrespectful. I apologizes."

"No need. I'm just so thankful I'm going to be part of this team."

"The Bureau is equally thankful for your service considering your unique skills with mathematics. I'll never understand how you were able stay out of the fray when Mr. Jinkowski's scheme went up in smoke. How is it he couldn't pull you in like he did everyone else?"

"I just said 'No' and he knew I was aware of where his skeletons were buried. I told him not to tell me anything about his monthly, four-hour stint in a locked office. I knew him when he was dating a friend of mine while he was still in school. He always was a corner-cutter and a first class louse! I was shocked when I applied for my position at Whitehouse Insurance and had to be interviewed by good old Jinksey. Maybe he thought I would just fall into step with his Bunco deals."

"Good…we're here." The limousine pulled into a dirty alley flanked by over-flowing trash barrels and broken down cardboard boxes leading to an underground garage of the most unpretentious building in sight. "Don't judge the offices by their exterior. I think you will be surprised. Old J. Edgar does nothing by halves!" *He would have liked to have added, "By eighths. A difficult, office layout – not conducive to quality work"* The hundred year old building stood in spite of the ravages on its bricks and mortar; no visible paint, no windows and an odor of decay.

They were escorted into an anti-room and told to begin filling out the papers found in yellow folders. Each folder had a current picture of the 'applicant' and a full biography, including education from kindergarten, military service, and employment records.

"I'll leave the three of you alone so you can fill out the forms."

The three just looked at each other. Eyes wide! The best Jac could come up with was, "If this doesn't beat all! Are the two of you sure you want to do this"

Janice was first to answer, "If I don't, who am I suppose to tell? And, wouldn't you think they could have given us some chairs or something to sit on, instead of having us stand at a shelf?"

"Good question. I was thinking the same thing. How about you Jac, how do you feel about things, so far?"

"Just like I did the night Janice drove me to the beach and pulled into a motel driveway, I didn't know that all she wanted to do was back out so she could find a parking place to view the ocean. I said to myself, 'if you have the money honey I've got the time.' So, it's the same for the FBI. I've got the time."

"How's it coming folks?" Agent Croft had entered the room."All you really have to do is sign the Acceptance form, then we'll get you fingerprinted and get some identification for you." He began to read from a folder in his hand. "Your physical is scheduled for nine in the morning. Report to the California Hospital at Fifteenth and Grand. You are scheduled for a full blood panel and general examination. This will allow each of you to have $1000 of life insurance, which by the way you can keep up after you finish with the bureau. If you have finished signing your acceptance we can go into our covert closet and discuss your function with the Bureau."

The three being lead down a hall looked very much like lambs to slaughter. *Jac couldn't help thinking how much this resembled his Navy Induction; Shut up, Walk here, Sign this.*

Ever cautious, Jac asked, "Why now?

"Regrettably, our Country is losing the scientific race of a life time! We need your help! You wouldn't be asked to place yourselves in harm's way. Once you are fully contracted to us we will establish 'secondary-bank accounts' to show Jac as a very successful attorney. Of course, you will in truth, continue in your chosen law path, and you, Janice, the office manager, with Em as legal investigator. By the way, how did you like the speed with which you received your Investigator's License?"

Grinning broadly, Em confessed how much the second chance meant to him, "This really means the beginning of a new life for me. I want all of you to know how much everything you've done means. All I can say is …you can count on me for 110 percent!"

∽

The covert closet was more a habitable room 'in progress' than the FBI 'secret' enclosure. It was doubtful the wall had ever been painted according to the obvious ravages on this 100 year old building. No windows. No carpets. A folding table and six chairs.

Agent Croft proffered a chair, "Here Miss Marrs, you sit here. Now then, I'm sure the three of you have several questions."

"More like a million!"

Jac appeared embarrassed, "Em, give the man a chance. We don't have to do anything we don't want to do, right Agent Croft?"

"Of course. Why don't you allow me to explain our mission and the part you can play in its completion. To begin with, let me share what the FBI is not allowed to do according to the many laws, regulations, and guidelines of our Federal Government. It neither prosecutes nor does it spy on Americans, contrary popular belief."

"You gott'a be kidding me!"

"Em, please! Try to remember that I'm an attorney and your boss. I'll say something if I think I need to question *anything!*"

Croft countered, "Em's okay, Jac. I understand how saturated many Americans have become by the rash of myths promulgated by both the press and movie industry about the functioning of the FBI. To tell you the truth, I was surprised to learn about some of the governing law I had misunderstood for years. So back to why you folks are here. First, We need information you folks learned regarding Mr. Brook's relationship to the Japanese he appears to have working for him. Second, the Department of Justice is interested in his realty holdings, here and abroad. If their information is even fifty-percent accurate, it would make him the third wealthiest man in the world. We want to learn … anything you know! How does that sit with you, considering he is passing himself off as a uncomplicated, insurance company president?"

After a short pause, Jac offered, "I think I understand what you would like from us. I wouldn't be surprised to know that the FBI learned of the 'missing second floor' when they investigated the Jinksey fiasco. That's probably when they asked you to change employers. Correct?"

"That's right, Jac. But not as easily accomplished as described. I've had some experience with saboteurs. The Bureau needed me and I needed 'outside' help. First, if you hadn't come by our State Office looking for a job when you did I would have included you and your friends in my general sweep of the Whitehouse offices. I remembered my first impression of you…commendable in view of your many accomplishments while in the military. Secondly, I reasoned it would be a shame to ruin a career before it had a chance to begin."

Em was hanging on every syllable. "Well, thank God for that, Jac. You saved both of us. Jeees, my wife would have divorced me. She wants that check every Friday!"

Jac couldn't control his unexpected, outburst of laughter, "Forgive me, but I can't help thinking that you haven't gotten a check from me *yet!"*

"Yah, but she loves *you*, especially since you gave her a job."

"Sorry about the interruption, Agent Croft. I'll contain myself."

"Not a problem. Please, call me AJ, and don't ask what the initials stand for or I'll have to kill you! Don't look like that, Em, that was just a joke!" Croft opened a case that had been sequestered under the table. These are outlines of what we need from you. Most of it has to do with what you've learned about the Japanese, so far."

"AJ, would you like to have me dictate the information. I'm learning to use the 'dreaded, sign of the times!' I'm supposing the office has such a dictating machine."

"We do, but most of the agents refuse to use it because it makes them embarrassed when someone listens to them while they are using it, but I'll be glad to get it for you. It **will** be much faster if you do that for us…thanks."

While Croft was out of the office the three began to chat in stage-whispers.

"Jac, you don't think we are being set-up, do you?"

"To do what, Em?"

"Gee, I don't know. But it seems to me the FBI is not in the habit of giving 'simple folks' like us this kind of opportunity."

"I hear you. But what you are forgetting is, we three have some very interesting information that I doubt anyone else has."

Janice repositioned herself in her chair...pulling her skirt well below her knees. "I agree with you, Jac! How do you want us to respond? I'm thinking he might want to separate us and if he does, how much should we say?"

"Stick to the truth. Neither the FBI nor the three of us have ever been in this situation before. Sit back and enjoy the ride! That's what the Navy always told me when I had a question. I'm like you. I like to be in control. At *all* times. Unfortunately, that isn't always possible!"

"Amen to that!" Em and Janice had answered in unison just as three men entered the room. One carried the dictating machine and the other two carried small folding tables and chairs.

"Folks, each of you can have your own table. This furniture is OLD ! Sorry about the rickety tables. At least this way, you won't bother each other as you fill-out your FBI badge information. Jac, you can go into a private room to dictate if you like."

"Thanks, anyway. I'll need my team to ensure accuracy. Three heads are better than one."

"Okay. I'm having some food sent in, what would you like to eat. I'd suggest you eat a big meal because we need to get you finger-printed and photographed after the paperwork is finished. May I take your orders now, or do you want to wait.?"

"What do you say, Team? I could eat now, how about you.?"

"Me, too!" In unison again.

"Name it and we will get it for you. Just write it down and don't forget soup, salad, drinks and dessert."

Em, couldn't restrain himself, "I like the FBI's style!"

༄

The next two hours past rather quickly for the trio. The food was well received by all. And, the report completed:

This report is the combined recollections of Braden Jacque Cartwright, LLB, Ms. Janice Marrs, and Mr. Emmery Gant, former Whitehouse Insurance Employee.

The afore mentioned did, as a team effort, follow initial curiosity when a hole was found in the insurance office of one Jason Alfred Brooks, President. Said hole exposed a second floor room not recognizable as present by current construction features. The room had about twenty persons(?) typing on silent, very small, green typewriters. The individuals had Japanese facial features.

A similar, 'second floor' was found in the office building behind the Wilshire Boulevard insurance building. The findings were the same, with one exception. A young man answered our knock at a third floor door, he appeared to be of Japanese descent, well bred, and well educated. The partly-opened door allowed an unobstructed view of the 'similar,' human-like figures bent over typewriters. In response to our questions, the typewriters were identified by his ' uncle' in a hand-written note, as Olivetti (from France or Italy); the word 'stop' was printed to the right of the word Olivetti. The young man said his uncle (who appeared to be in charge of the production) was not certain about their origin. A personal aside: First, the young man sounded as though he might be a recent visitor to Los Angeles. Second, the workforce did not appear human...more mechanical.

Respectfully,

Dictated by: B. J. Cartwright Time/ Dated 3:57 P.M. March 26, 1949

Agent Croft nodded with a smile, then turned toward Janice, "The Bureau Supervisor would like to speak to you in the next room."

"Do I need an attorney to accompany me?"

"Not this time." Smiling, Croft led her to the door.

ᢞ

"Great to see you girl! I've really missed you... all of you!"

25. The Reunion

Janice gave her FBI *boss* a look that said *'what's going on?'* "Isn't this dangerous. Won't Croft catch a drift that something other than Bureau business is on your mind?"

The Supervisor physically moved her to the far end of the large room."You don't look very happy to be back in the office, Janice. I thought you would be pleased to hear the great things the Pentagon is saying about your accomplishments. And, in so short a time. My God, they tell me you did everything in a little over a week! Is that true?"

Janice looked less than pleased, "I can't stand that 'shit-eating- grin' of yours! Let's cut to the chase! You can't wait to put this case 'to bed' so you can take all the credit and get your three dollar statue at the Joint Chiefs' Luncheon! I smell a retirement in the offing! You lied to me, you low-life!"

The Supervisor took hold of Janice's shoulders to pull her to him. The sound of a distant telephone caused his body to shift with a sudden jerk. He put his finger to his lip and whispered, "The place is still *hot,* and soon there will be cameras installed. I'd better put this on hold until we can be in a better place."

Janice was instantly relieved. She spoke in a louder voice, "So when do you expect to retire? And, why was I called back to the office? I thought we had agreed that I would stay clear until I had a clear bead on who and what Mr. Jacques is in 'reality.' I'm in no way finished with my investigation! As for Mr. Croft, formerly of the State Board of Insurance Regulators, I'm not impressed! He probably shined his family's shoes every Saturday night in order that all 'I's were dotted and 'T's crossed before church. He's about as dull as last year's news! If he has an angle it's to do good for others. He's the last of the real, tried and true, 'do-gooders!' I'll go to the bank on that one!"

"Don't bet the farm! He's up to something, I just don't know what. The Brethren are concerned. They had hoped you would have some 'intelligence' for us, at least, more than 'he's just a do-gooder.' They are sure someone has found the Concordia! You know what that will mean, if true! Our Country could become a pawn in a global game it can *never* win!"

"I don't have to be reminded! Besides, I didn't think you wanted me to lie. I thought Jac was the one you plan to bring into the Cabal. I'm doing my best with him."

"I'll bet you are! The two of your almost looked quite 'cozy' as I watched through one-way glass."

Janice's eyes flashed with a mixture of anger and delight, "My poor, poor, Boss is jealous! That's really *too* bad!"

"You seem to take great comfort from my dis-comfort! Why? Isn't it enough that I have to read and report all transmissions of your comings and goings with that man? There are times when I feel sure you are just using me. And, I'll be DAMNED if I can reason why! I guess I'm just getting what I deserve. Our manual warns against fraternization. Fraternization, HELL! I'm gone on you and you know it! I hate it! I wish I could change the urges!"

"I'm not doing any of the things you have accused me of doing. If I played the 'coquet' with you from time to time it was because it made me feel alive for just that second or two. It made me feel like a real woman, not just an actor on a stage. Do you have any idea how much I hate lying to people just so I can get information. Or, have to change my behavior when it fits Agency needs? Of course, that was before Jac! I'm really a decent person, and want to do my part! But there are times when I have to wonder if what I'm doing has ANY impact on National Defense. I think what I really need is a vacation from all of you!"

"Who knows, maybe you and Jac can take one. We are sending the two you to where he was born, that should wrap-up our 'pre-lim' on him. All kidding aside, I think he will make a fine agent...for both organizations!. And, if there is anything between yo..."

Mimicking The Supervisor, Janice interrupted in a very loud voice, "AND, IF THERE IS ANYTHING BETWEEN THE TWO OF YOU!" Janice abruptly interrupted herself, "Who's *we,* and what are you talking about? You really have a nerve!"

"Hold it down! You didn't even allow me to finish my sentence." Walking toward the bugging device he had replaced on the table he said in a stern, but muffled voice, "I'm still your boss, and I call the shots. I expect you will allow me the appropriate respect due me and my office!" He put his finger to his lips, once again and pointed towards the innocent looking bunch of dried flowers on the table. "I'm so happy to see you again, Miss Marrs. I've learned of your potential, and I'm positive you will continue to find the Bureau much to your liking. Tell me, how long have you been in Los Angeles?"

A wry smile crossed her face, "I thought you knew all about us!" Janice looked him straight in the eyes, "Let's get back to business! When do Jac and I leave for Illinois? And, WHO is 'WE?'"

"Very soon, in fact, in the morning. The three of you will receive your packets in the morning. You change planes in Chicago and take a puddle-jumper to Quincy. A car will be waiting. Jac still has an Illinois license. He'll do the driving Beware of his old man, I understand he's a 'butt-patter.' His mom is an enigma, our best intelligence says she is a deceptive character. Vapid one moment, discerning in another. She sounds well read, but lacks social maturity. She seems to thinks that all she has to do is smile, head cocked to one side and all bad things will disappear. Including her husband. Jac is her favorite. The other two kids get what's left of any maternal feeling. All I'm saying is, walk carefully and carry your gun.

"I'm opposed to that! You know I'm not comfortable when I'm 'carrying!'"

"You'll be less comfortable if there are any 'n's in the wood pile.'"

"Since when did you stop saying nigger? I thought it was one of your favorite words."

"Since the Bureau decided we should change our image, we have to say, colored people. Some damn person is doing a research called a 'survey' and found we were thought to be like the KKK. Doesn't that just take all!"

"It couldn't hurt. I don't like to see people taken advantage of just because of their skin color. Remember the time you had me out in Watts working in the small bakery. Remember how angry I was when you wouldn't let me come in, and I had to sell pumpkin pies that had green mold that was taken off with a knife and sold for sweet potato pies? Two days was too much for me! I'm glad I've been advanced in grade. I couldn't take any more of that!"

The Supervisor addressed Janice in a voice that said he hadn't hear a word she had spoken in the last five minutes. "When you arrive you will be met by Agent Riddle, ostensibly a tenant farmer in the area who just got off your plane and heard your destination. He will present as, 'also going to Warsaw and might he hitch a ride.' Your code is "hopscotch.""

"I just have two things to say, first, you are a weasel…too afraid to give out the information about the trip, don't ask me why! Second, I thought you told me "Hopscotch" was a dead 'program.' What happened?"

"Not now, I'll tell you more later. Promise."

"You still haven't answered MY question! WHO is 'WE?' The FBI or the Brethren?"

෴

26. Croft's Plan's

Croft finished reading Jac's report, "Really good work!, Probably some of the best I've ever read, of course, the State Department rarely had need for such a succinct report. Something like this usually comes much later. But, again, good work! The FBI is in your debt!" Croft carefully placed the report onto a silver folder and placed it into a large brown envelope.

"Are we free to go?"

"What's wrong Emmery, anxious to leave?"

"No way, Cro…, pardon, Mr. Croft! Just can't think of how we can be help to you since you know every-thing we know."

"Believe it or not, each of you is extremely impor-tant to us!" *Croft chuckled, then broke into a broad grin.* "Don't you realize the three of you are PER-FECT! We need people with no negative, 'stand-out' history."

Em interrupted. "What about Jac? He's a real hero!"

"Very true. No disrespect intended. It's just that the three of you are like three, uncut diamonds, rough around the edges, but each with a special talent. Jac

147

you are very approachable. You look young enough to be everyone's big brother. And, if I didn't know you better, and I had to find a 'subject' for our current problem, I would say you could be sold Lady Liberty herself! I know you are not as naïve as you appear. Janice is beautiful, brainy, without academic laurels, with an uncanny ability to 'read' people. I seriously doubt her 'bar' experience is her only rub with abstract reasoning and education. Few have her capacity for recognizing exceptional human quality and moral judgment!" She will serve the Bureau handsomely!"

"Wai..wait.....a minute! I thought this was a one-time-only affair! What have I signed-up for? Hey, Jac! What's going on?"

Jac looked a bit sheepishly as he turned toward Em. "Why don't we wait until Mr. Croft has a chance to explain exactly what it is he has in mind. I must admit I'm more than a little confused myself. I do have an office to return to before the rent is due." *Jac offered a poor excuse for a joke –provoked laugh, as he faced Croft.*

"This is what we know about the three of you. You love your country. Hate bigotry. Make every effort to help others. *With what Em classified as ' a shit-eating-grin' on his face as he turned to face Em,* "Or, perhaps helped yourself a bit along the way. Basically, you are all straight arrows with a deep moral regard for human rights. Just the kind of folks this organization needs! Especially, now."

"Now, because? Jac asked.

"Now, because as I said before, our Country is facing the race of a lifetime, and regrettably, we are losing at the present. That's why we need all of you! Enough of that! Let's get to your schedules for the next three days." He handed each of them a typed list.

"Boy, are we going to be busy! I need to tell you I faint at the sight of needles!"

"Em, I will see to it you don't hit your head." Everyone had a good laugh at Em's concern for his health in the hospital. "Team, it seems we had better be taken home. Did you know it was ten o'clock?"

"Yah, and we haven't eaten in hours." Em spoke for everyone. "Our car will have you back in thirty-minutes." Croft turned toward Jac, "See the three of you at the hospital in the morning."

Jac looked toward the closed door, "I wonder what's taking Janice so long? Who is this Supervisor? What can he want with her.?"

"Sorry, Jac, I haven't the foggiest!"

"It's a good thing Tiny Naylor's was open. I'm starved!" Janice left little room for questions, she lead the three friends (cohorts, and un-cover agents of the FBI) to their favorite booth to review of the day's events.

27. Em's Wife

In spite of the hour, Em had a desperate need to tell someone. He knew full well the admonition to remain silent on the subject of "Bureau Agent!" The moniker alone gave impetus to his anxiety! He believed his wife *would never tell.* She was good at keeping secrets! The house was dark when Emmery arrived home, or so he thought. He knew better than to leave his briefcase near the door; the closet was only a few steps away. Before he could make the closet door his wife fled the kitchen, nearly knocking him over.

"What's going on? Why no lights? I know it's late, but you always wait up!"

Before his wife could answer, a back door slammed. Em was certain he had seen the figure of a man run down the drive.

"My, God! Are you having an affair?"

"Get a grip, Stupid! Do I look like a person who would be having an affair?" Her stocky frame remained unmoved. Her folded arms told him to 'drop it!"

The snap of over-head lights gave Em a clear look at the woman he married twenty years ago. Squat, dish-water, blonde, unkempt, with an unceasing, staccato voice that could be heard for a block away! How was it he had never really taken a good look? Was she always like this? *Clarisa Mae Gant, you **are** more than a caution!*

Remembering how happy she seemed to be when she was asked to work with the office trio, Em Asked, "What happened to the woman who was eager to join forces with the three of us? You sound like a total stranger."

As quickly as the light had appeared, Clarisa reverted to the role Em had always found familiar. "Don't pay any attention to me tonight, I've had an awful scare!"

"My God! What happened? Did that man hurt you? Was he a burglar?

"No! He was some kind of government agent. Could be FBI for all I know."

Em went white. He could only muster, "I very much doubt it!" He remembered that Croft said not to tell her anything. "What did he want? And, why was he in our bedroom?"

"Well, you may doubt it all you want, but I'm telling you he was some kind of government agent! And, as for the bedroom, he said he was looking for bugs. He made me mad when he laughed after I said I used bug spray every month. You can stop smiling! You don't know what I have been through today!"

Em noticed Clarisa was holding something in her hand. "What have you got in your hand?"

"Don't ask me to explain! It just doesn't make any sense. He called it a "lagger" and said I should show it if I ever get in trouble. Here you take it!"

"Are you kidding me? What the hell is it. It almost looks like a cross."

"You're right! Then he said I should remember "hopscotch," and that's when I remembered the kid's game I used to play! I needed a "lagger" so I could play. I would throw a chain or rock, or anything that would not go out of bounds."

"Yah. I think I remember the game. But what's that got to do with your 'visitor?' The whole thing sounds fishy to me. Did he give you a card or something with a telephone number?"

"No. I thought that was strange *too*. He just ske-daddled when he heard you come in. What do you think it's all about?"

"Beats me, but I know someone I can ask" *Being careful not to reveal his secret – he lied.* "I'll ask Jac, he'll tell us what to do. You can bet on that! Again! Go to bed!"

ᏉᎩ

"I'm sorry I couldn't call before now, my husband just left for work."*Clarisa listens for a moment.* "No, he doesn't suspect anything. Of course I was care-ful. I only told him what you told me to tell him; 'the man was looking for bugs in the bedroom told me to remember "hopscotch."* Clarissa listens carefully to the instructions being given to her.* "Yes, I have everything. I've been writing on my notepad. "DON'T SCREAM AT ME! Of course I have a brain in my head! Who do you think you are to speak to me in that tone? Frankly, I don't give a tinker's damn who you represent! And that's final!"

Following a very long period of listening, Clarisa nods her head 'yes' and promises to keep the agent fully informed of any suspicious behaviors in Jac's office. She forgot to tell her "contact" that her husband was planning to ask Jac for advice about the 'visitor.'

28. Trip To Warsaw

Em arrived at the office some thirty minutes early. He heard a key in the lock which reminded him he had forgotten to leave the door open.

"Sorry, Guys! Should have left it open for you. I'm just a little wacky – thinking about the hospital and the needles!" He opened the door, "Oh, I thought you were the boss."

"It's okay mister, I'm just delivering a package. Sign here."

The package held a packet for each of the 'three musketeers;' lengthy instructions, plane tickets, pocket money, and Agency Identification Surety cards.

When Janice and Jac walked in, Em asked, "Where the hell is Warsaw, Illinois?"

Jac laughed out loud, "At the Mississippi River Bottoms! And I do mean "bottoms!"

It took the better part of an hour to digest the infor-mation. The partners discussed personal reserva-tions each held for the prospect of working for the Bureau. No salutations, just questions! "And, what was going to happen to the hospital appointments?"

"And, further, why didn't Croft mention all of this last night?" Both fellows thought that for a girl, Janice was more relaxed about the entire proceedings, both yesterday and today. "And, why did she spend so much time away from them when she was in the other Bureau office?"

Em was the first to speak. "Hey, Girl, is there anything you aren't telling us? After all, you did go into a room with someone other than our Mr. Croft and stayed a very long time."

Jac agreed, "Are you keeping something from us?"

Janice was prepared for the questions and had been given permission to tell Jac the reason they would be going to Warsaw.

"You've got to be kidding. They want me to be an attorney for the FBI?"

"Sorry, Jac. Not an attorney, an undercover agent."

Em jumped up from his chair, "He'd be lousy, I'd be perfect! Are you certain they didn't include me?"

Janice thought Em was about to cry, "It seems that the Bureau prefers single men." *She gave a heavy 'girly' sigh.* "Darn it. They want to take all the fun out of everything."

Jac was obviously in deep thought. He hadn't hear Janice's explanation. "How is it they told you about why we were going on this trip and not me?"

"Damn good question if you ask me. I'd like to know too."

"Don't ask me fellows, I was told by the Supervisor, when the three of us were escorted out of the office with Mr. Croft!"

"Why didn't you tell me last night?" Jac sounded offended.

"Simple! Because I was told to tell you this morning after the packets arrived."

"I still don't understand."

Em spoke up, "Forget it! I've got bigger questions!" Now that he had every ones full attention! He only needed five minutes to deliver a rapid fire, blow by blow, of the strange events from last night. His addition to the story caught Jac'c attention to every detail. "So, what do you guys think? And, what's this thing called "hopscotch," and the 'lagger' thing, don't speak all at once! Don't either of you have any ideas?"

Janice weakly offered, "Oh, it's probably nothing. Maybe your wife made up the story to keep you 'interested.' How can a kid's game be of any importance, anyway?" *This was getting too close for comfort of any description. Janice could only hope her cover sounded plausible.*

"Not on your life, Janice! You don't know my wife. She doesn't have a creative bone in her body, much less entertain a man in our bedroom! She'd want to do it in front of the neighbors."

"Okay, you two. Enough is enough. Why don't we get the encyclopedia and check out the game of Hopscotch." *He decided against telling the pair about his last conversation with Doc Harks. Jac held his questions for a more opportune time and place.*

"Fellas, I think this will have to wait. Did you notice the departure time on your tickets?"

"See, Em, now you know why I love her; always taking care of details" Jac blew her an air-kiss.

"By the way, why do you suppose they have us staying in Iowa, I thought we were going to be in Illinois."

Jac patted his friend's shoulder, "Fear not, We are staying in Keokuk, Iowa because it is just across the river from Warsaw, and has the only hotel. And, as a treat you will see and hear the Delta Queen as she ties up long enough to take on passengers and stores for her trip south. I'll bet you've never heard a paddle boat with a calipee. It can make a fellow homesick." *A short pause,* "Almost – homesick."

∽

Janice was the first to speak when the little plane landed. "It's going to take a month to get the kinks out of my neck, that was the smallest, most uncomfortable 'thing' I've ever ridden in!"

"I told you it would be a puddle-jumper!"

"How do you know those things? You've never ridden on one before, have you?"

Em's face seemed to have colored a bit, "Common sense tells you that connector or commuter planes have to do a lot of work with little space."

"Jac, I'm sure you are used to all this, but, PLEASE GOD…can we go home some other way?"

∽

29. The Truth

The hotel café had just opened. The counter by the
coffee urn was jammed with river jockeys and swamp
buddies, waiting for a first cup to start the day. Janice
met Jac with a small hug as they made their way to
a table at the rear of the room. The old fixtures gave
the place a museum look. Thick marble back-bar,
and sparkling ten-foot mirrors lined a twenty-foot wall.
Ages old soda glasses appeared to weigh at least,
two or three pounds apiece.

"Jac, I hate getting up this early! But I hate this
hotel more! Are your bed springs as lopsided and
noisy as mine?"

"Yes! Remember, I told you this was the only hotel
for miles? Before we meet Em I want an opportunity
to talk to you. I have a dozen question I want to ask!"
Jac took Janice by the shoulders, "Janice. I'm really
serious! I want the truth. And, I want it now."

"Okay, Jac, you asked for it." Her body sagged
just a moment, then returned to a more natural pose.
An additional pause, "I don't know any more than
you do."

"Get off of it! Who did you meet when we were at the FBI office" And, why did you get all the information about this trip, whatever it's supposed to be?" And, who are WE? You, for sure, are not the same person who was so helpful and sweet! I'll ask it again, why are we here?"

"Jac, all I was told was that the Bureau though you might make a great undercover agent. And, that's the truth!" Janice moved to Jac's chair, sat very close to him, held his cheeks with both hands and gave him a soft, gentle kiss. She became aware of Jac's physical acknowledgment of her advances. She knew this was not the time to risk the assignment by pursuing Jac's *rare* response. Further, Em was about to join them.

᠙

Breakfast had little to offer the three tired, body-aching, "soldiers." No one spoke a word. The drive to the "homestead" was bumpy, dirty, and a major labor for the rented Chevrolet.

"Hey, Jac, how did you say you got away from this God forsaken place?"

"Em, it's not like you to talk like that," Janice admonished.

"What's happened?" Both of you, stop it!" Jac was adamant, "I don't know what we are doing here, but whatever it is, just don't make fun of my home or my folks, no matter how stupid you think they are! I'll do that myself, not you! Is that clear?"

In unison, "yes, Jac." *Neither had ever seen this side of Jac, nor had they ever heard such a scornful tone during any of their previous conversations.*

"Good, now what are we supposed to do once we get there? You said we each had a different assignment. Tell us about yours, Janice. Mine just says to visit the folks, spend a little time with Shep, and wait for the two of you to return…then leave."

Em interrupted, "I have the best assignment! All I have to do is find a geode. I guess there must be a thousand of them here near the creek you spoke of – right? And when I return…"change my shoes and place them into the bag provided." It doesn't make sense to me, but who cares about what I think. I'm just glad to get away from the wife, even if only for a day!"

"Don't count you chickens …"

Em, interrupted,, "I know, before they hatch!

"Right! Let's talk about your…important assignment. Only God knows why! You need to know what they look like if you want to find any. It's not real easy. Geodes just look like dirty rocks. You have to crack them open to see the beauty. And, 'cracking' is no easy chore! You have to throw them down on a rock, really hard. If it opens, you have a real beauty in hand. I never cease to wonder at the magic of a geode. Now, about the short vacation from your wife…enjoy it while you can. There could be trouble ahead." Jac turned, "How, about you, Janice? What's planned for you?"

Janice opened her packet and read, "Go to the Depot Hotel…alone. Use the enclosed tape to draw a schematic, as close to perfect, as possible. Include every wall, nook, and cranny! Leave nothing out of your drawing."

Jac broke the long pause, "Why would anyone want that kind of information about a building that is at least 150 years old. It's probably ready to fall apart. Please be careful. I think I should go with you."

"I don't think you are suppose to. The Supervisor said I was to go alone. God knows why. I've never been here before!" *One more lie couldn't do any harm.*

The three continued the drive to the Cartwright home in silence.

∽

Five minutes unto the 'hellos' Jac's dad complained about not being told there would be any one coming to visit. *Jac's dad never did like "company," he said they ate too much and stayed too late.* Jac's mom said she was pleased to meet every one and hoped they would visit again; turned, and walked away. Dad followed. *Jac was stunned!* Jac's sister was 'somewhere' according to mother. Her words had been short and sweet and to the point! A completely new behavior for her, according to Jac's recollection. The trio stood on the hard-packed earth like garden statues waiting for rain. The parents hurried toward a tangle of weeds and trees.

Janice was the first to make a move. After getting directions to the hotel, she caught up with, and hugged Mrs. Cartwright, gave a quick pat to Mr. Cartwright's shoulder and made her way to the abandoned Depot Hotel. *I should be back in about twenty minutes.* "Bye, Guys! See you at the car."

Jac's dad met them before they could complete their assignments, "What in the hell does she think she's going to do when she gets there? There's nothing out there except the old, abandoned Hotel. It closed right after you left, Jac. Some government guys came here one morning, handed me a Government Closure paper and one thousand dollars, and asked for the keys to the hotel.

For the thousand, I would have thrown in your sister AND your mother...if they wanted!"

Em looked incredulous, "He's kidding, right?"

Dad answered for himself, "In a pig's eye! Chances like that don't come around every day!."

For Jac, this was worse than his out-of-body experience in the war. Nothing was 'right!' His parents sounded like strangers. Acted like strangers. Jac could only wonder to himself how he could have ever thought this rude, crass, man intelligent. He had never been so embarrassed in his life. And, his mother? Was she taking drugs? He could feel his face become red hot. He needed to leave...now! Jac called out, "It was nice to see you and mom...I think. I have to tell you I feel like I have wandered into a Buck Rogers serial! I hope I am able to wake up from this nightmare."

Jac waited for his dad to say something, any-thing! Nothing came. Not a word. Not a 'goodbye,' not even a 'go to hell!' *Jac was sure something was very wrong. Dad, semi- normal, mom like a zombie, and sis nowhere in sight! Not at all like mom! The others, ...well...maybe!*

Needing an excuse to leave, Jac took hold of Em's arm. "If you want to find a real geode, I'll go with you." The two men reached the creek bed and began hunt-ing.

"Jac! Come here! I think I found one! Look!" Em held a heavy (for him), ugly, gray rock.

"Good for you! Now slam it down on a couple of rocks."

"Okay. Here goes." It took four tries. Finally, Em had his treasure; beautiful amethyst crystals lining the interior of the dirty, grey rock. "Let's get this back to the car. This rock is beautiful, but I wonder why I was supposed to get it?"

"I wonder too! Maybe Janice can fill is in on the mystery. She seems to know everything! Especially, since she left us alone with Croft at the Bureau office."

"I have to agree, Jac. She hasn't been the same since."

"I'm sure you didn't fall for that bit about me becoming an undercover agent. What a 'load' that was!"

"You don't think that's why we are here? But, Jac, remember when Croft said you might become some kind of an attorney for the FBI? Maybe that's the rea-son."

"Not on your tin type! Janice has something up her sleeve! And, I plan to find out what it is!"

They had been waiting quietly in the car for some ten minutes before Em spoke, "I wish we could turn back the clock to four days ago when we were having such a great time getting settled in our new office! Do you think we will ever be allowed to return ?"

"You bet we will! I'm still in charge of my own life, and yours if that's still what you want!"

"You bet it is, Jac! We're a team!"

"Hey, Fella's, I'm back!" Note pad in hand and a skinned knee, Janice regaled the men with information of the most mundane sort. "I was told to draw a schematic of the old hotel. It's a good thing I was given a map, otherwise I would probably still be wandering through the old relic. It must be near two hundred years old. I've never seen such beautiful wood. It think that place will stand erect for the next hundred years! While I was in there, Jac, I tried to imagine how you filled your days inside and outside of the hotel. I remembered you said you spent much of your time hunting squirrels, and helping your mother. After the greeting we received this morning, I'm surprised you took so long to escape! Your mom really surprised me! I expected a fragile, genteel, southern type, women who, above all, would exude 'courtesy.' There wasn't much of that in the greeting. There's nothing about you that fits this place! Maybe your were adopted! Any way, you won't believe what I found! Someone must have needed a place to hide some printing stuff! There's scads of it! God knows why."

Jac lamented, having heard nothing Janice had said, "If only they had paid my dad a lot of money years ago! My life would have been different!" In a poor attempt to make a joke, Jac said, "Who knows I could'a been'a 'hep' kiddo!"

Janice couldn't help herself, "It's "cat" not "kiddo!" Gee, Jac, half-Italian and half-hipster! You crack me up, Jac!"

The three friends enjoyed a hearty laugh, something they needed before getting down to the business of comparing notes on their strange, 'go nowhere adventure,' as Em had complained. The return to Los Angeles was... thankfully, uneventful. Each promised to meet for breakfast in the morning. Em went home to his wife. Jac and Janice spoke of Jac's new apartment. Jac's inability to find the appropriate words for the moment gave Janice the opportunity to give Jac a friendly hug and ask, "Should I go to my place?"

"No." Jac's singular reply.

Janice brightened, smiling ear to ear, pledged to cook a great meal for the two of them.

"No need to cook, I'll get some stuff from Nat's Deli. That will give us a chance to compare notes on what is happening to the three of us, and what we can do about it!" *Jac's countenance created an unseen wedge between the two of them.*

Jac turned and was about to leave when Janice asked, "Is information the only thing I'm good for? I thought we were building a relationship that could become a 'for-ever-more' experience for both of us. Was I wrong?"

Once again Jac was burning from embarrassment. "You're not wrong … exactly. It's just I'm so confused at the moment it hard to know how I feel about anything."

"Well, how about if we move together and save money for the future, I'll bet THAT would interest you!

Janice's heart sank when she heard a muffled, "Okay."

30. What's In A Name

The office 'trio' arrived at the restaurant at the same time, sat in the booth they usually selected, and ordered the same breakfast.

Em was the first to speak, "Boy, there's nothing like a day in the country to bring out the "happy juices" in folks!"

"That's enough of that, Em. We don't need it right now!"

"Well, for what it's worth, I think Em has a great point! You've been in a real snit since we left Illinois, Jac!"

"All right, Janice! All right! I'll be just fine as soon as I get some answers to my questions."

Not to feel left-out, Em offered, "It sounds like the two of you are having a private conversation; should I leave?"

"No!"

"Gee, Jac that was…succinct!"

Em interrupted, "This sounds like a private fight, can't it wait until we get to the office? Better still, let's just take a breath and focus on digesting our food."

This was an unexposed side of Em. He sounded more professorial than investigator. Jac and Janice looked up in surprised. *Jac thought to himself, "It's not enough not to know who Janice is, now I've got the 'true' Em to wonder about!"*

∽

The office must have held a sense of "safe harbor" because the three of them were smiling when Jac closed the office door behind them.

"Please, let's turn back the clock and pretend Craft never called us to the Bureau! I don't know about the two of you…I'm ready to do some business for just us!"

Again, Janice and Em agreed in unison.

"Great! Let's check the mail and see what we have." Jac felt more relieved, and hoped the cloud of questions lingering over his head about Janice would disappear.

"Janice, I'm with you." Em added. "I think you and I should answer Jac's questions before we do anything else."

"That's fine with me, if Jac agrees."

"Of course, I agree! And, that would suit me fine. I'm ready to get back to the wonderful plans I had for us! I guess the only way to get my questions out of our way is to start!"

The questions lasted well into the late afternoon. No break for lunch, and no suggestions for supper. Jac had Janice take notes on the information each shared. On review, it became obvious Jac questioned the Bureau's true intensions in having the three "help." Jac couldn't understand what the 'missing' second floor of Whitehouse Insurance Company had to do with Warsaw, Illinois, and of Janice making a schematic of the Depot Hotel. Then there was Em and his geode, and more disturbingly, Jac's mother's trance-like behavior. And, what had she meant when she told Jac to play "hopscotch?" Hopscotch was a girl's game! Why would she say that? *Once again, bringing Doc Harks to mind. Did Mom have a 'lagger' too?*

"And, before we finish, I have one last question. Janice, why did you refer to the Bureau as the "Agency" when I asked you how it was that you were given information the two us had to wait overnight to receive?"

Em chimed in, "I wondered about that as well." *Em was still in his (newly acquired?) 'voice.'*

"Em I don't know what to tell the two of you. It just happened that way. The man called me to the other room and asked a few questions, and according to his 'for the sake of brevity and your personal time' reeled off the information and said the three of us could discuss it when the two of you received your packets. I guess he didn't think I could remember everything. And, as for the use of "agency," I guess I just think the two names, agency and bureau are interchangeable." *Janice proved to have a colossal, capacity for lying. She was very pleased with herself since she thought she could see Jac relax his jaw that had remained taut for the last twenty-four hours. She had to admit she had real feeling for Jac and didn't want her "assignment" to hurt him in any way. He was still the 'best' she had ever met! In truth, she too had questions about the Illinois trip. Who was responsible? The FBI or the Cabal? Her gut said, "None of the above! Probably a personal ploy, whereby The Supervisor could utilize the FBI to achieve a personal objective! Janice was at a loss to explain how the 'latter' felt so right!*

The office phone rang. "I'll get it!" Janice hurried to answer. *Pause* "Good Morning, Agent Croft. Yes, I'll be happy to get Jac."

Jac remained quiet as he heard Croft share his concern about their safety when he was unable to contact anyone of the three; as had been prearranged. "What happened? Where were you? You'll never know how much I worried the Japanese had gotten a hold on the three of you!"

"Jac stammered a response, "I,..... I..I guess I thought you would have been told."

Janice grabbed the phone from Jac, "Hi, Agent Croft! Good to hear from you! I guess you weren't told about the "side" assignment that could help Jac become an undercover agent."

"I have to admit that I had no idea Jac wanted to become a permanent agent. When did he get the "Idea? Croft asked.

"Oh, I don't really know, maybe it came as a surprise to him. Who knows. Anyway, the Supervisor wanted us to help with some of the preliminaries. But here we are...ready to help in any way possible!"

"Good." *Croft couldn't quell the uneasy feeling that rose higher than it had, when Janice stayed in the Supervisor's office. He began to piece together the bits of information that partially explained his assignment, "Keep your eyes OPEN! Report any questions that develop about the Supervisor's behavior. Oral report, only!"*

Janice could hear the disbelief in Croft's voice. She only hoped she had "covered" well enough to dispel any further investigation of the absence. *The Supervisor is going to ream me out on this one.* She hung up the phone.

"What in the name of Jehovah was that all about? You amaze me, Janice! You lie like a rug!"

"I agree with you Jac!" Em was incredulous. "Why was it necessary to lie when the trip was a result of a Bureau request? Is there something you aren't telling us? Relieve yourself of the burden, we're going to know now or later, it's up to you!"

Jac's knuckles were white, He looked as though he were about to explode. "I'm not going to move a muscle until I get a full explanation! What is going on with you and this "supervisor? Is he Bureau or not? Wait! Wait a ... minute! Is he a double-agent?"

"Don't be ridiculous, Jac! Where did that idea come from? You're brighter than that!"

"Not so fast, Janice." Em was calculating the possibilities. "It's not such a crazy idea. It could make good sense, except for one factor. You, Janice, would also need to be a "double-agent. I have to admit, I can't even guess 'whose double-agent' you might be! So .... what is the answer?"

"What's happened to the 'three friends?' One phone call and now we are nothing more than enemies?" Janice move to a chair in the corner. "I guess I need to come clean. If both of you promise not to laugh." *Janice's mind race a mile a minute. She knew she would have to lie; in her mind, the safety of the Country depended on her ability satisfy both Friends!* Or, so she thought.

Both men moved closer. They wanted to insure they heard every word spoken.

"First, the investigation that took us to Illin ..."Janice was interrupted by loud pounding on the office door.

"Come ON, open the DAMN door," The booming voice could have been heard at street level! Everyone remained frozen in place. "God Damn It, I KNOW YOU ARE IN THERE!"

"Jeeze, it sounds like Brooks!" Em was white as new snow.

"If you want to enter you will have to change your demeanor. UNDERSTAND!" Jac had about all he could tolerate today. "Is that you, Mr. Brooks?"

"GOD DAMN RIGHT!"

Jac took no prisoners, "Come back when you cool off!" Everyone was silent, including Brooks. After a minute or two, "Are you ready to come in PROPERLY"

"Yeh, yeh, open the door!" A dirty, disheveled, unshaven, partially-dressed man stood before them. "Got any coffee?"

Jac was the first to speak, "When did you eat last?"

"I don't remember. It doesn't matter! I just want you to be my attorney! I'm not kidding. Just say 'yes! I'm in a hurry!"

"You know me better than that, Mr. Brooks. I need to know why you need an attorney. Does it have anything to do with the two 'missing' second floors. Especially, the one you were spying on through the hole in your office?"

"You DUMB KID! Why else?"

"Then I suggest you take my advice, contact the FBI, and offer to assist in their investigation." *Brooks sank into his chair like a deflated balloon.* "Em, call Mr. Croft. Tell him a friend would like to help him."

"Jac, Croft wants to talk to you."

"Thanks, Mr. Croft ...sorry, AJ, I think we need to get together as soon as possible. First, I want to feed Mr. Brooks before you come over. Or, am I assuming too much, to think that you would want to come to my office? Good! Would you like to eat with us, we need food...now. Great, I'll order-in. Chinese, Okay?"

∽

31. The Real Assignment?

Brooks eagerly drank his soup, gobbled chicken wings… bones and all, and drank two containers of sola before relaxing in his chair. The four observers could only guess how Brooks had survived for the last few days.

Agent Croft was the first to speak, "Brooks, I'm glad you've decided to assist the Bureau in sorting out the strange goings-on at Whitehouse Insurance. I am curious why you haven't sought out a friend or two to help you? At least, give you a place to stay and some-thing to eat?"

"What friends?"

The four sets of eyes met in recognition of what this 'famous tycoon' was admitting. Croft, continued, "I didn't mean to intrude into your private life, Mr. Brooks."

"Sure you didn't! How much is it going to cost me to get things straight? That's all I want to know! I tried to get Cartwright to represent me but he's such a tight ass he has to be assured he won't get his lily-white hands a little dirty."

"I don't blame him, Mr. Brooks. I can promise you that your civil liberties WILL NOT be abridged in any fashion. All we, the Bureau, want is information about the Japanese in your building."

"You mean I still own it? What kind of a trick is this?"

"No trick. All we need is information. Nothing can be taken from you unless there is a successful, legal action taken against you. I would have imagined you understood the workings of our legal system."

"I don't know what I know. I haven't slept in three days, and everything's still a jumble!"

Everyone remained silent as Brooks, slumped in his chair began to snore.

∽

Within an hour Brooks had been picked up by local Bureau Agents; leaving the three office mates to sort out the remaining situation. Jac began pacing, "I can think better when I walk around. Okay? This is how I see it. The Bureau has Brooks so we are out of it! They don't need our help for anything...thank God! What say we get on with the business of setting up OUR business? We have real live clients who haven't heard from us!"

Janice began to laugh, "Jac, do you realize that you've only been in LA three weeks?"

"My God, you are right! How can that be?"

"Welcome to the Big City, fella!"

"Yah, thanks, I really needed that, Em! Keep me in the 'present.' I hate! No, dislike people how keep talking about the way it was 'back home,' but this is really nothing like back home!"

Janice felt left out, but not to the point where it would be worth starting a row, "If the two men in this office would like to get some work accomplished ...i'd"

Jac interrupted, "Right you are, as usual, Angel." *He felt more comfortable than he had in days. Even though he still held deep reservation about some of Janice's behaviors.* "What's first on the proverbial docket?"

"My God, Janice, he called you, "Angel!" Things must be improving between the two of you."

Jac pretended to ignore both of them, "I think we should make a list of questions to ask AJ about the trip we took to Warsaw; then we can set up a new office calendar."

"Why do we have to ask any questions, Jac? I don't know what the trip had to do with Agent Croft...if anything?" *There was an edge to her voice.*

"Janice, once and for ALL, what is it you are NOT saying? I want to know... NOW!"

"Hey, Guys! Leave me out of this. I get enough of this at home, I don't need more from the office." Em got up to leave.

"Please sit down." Jac was embarrassed. "I don't know what's wrong with me. It's just that something seems out of place and I can't put my finger on it! I don't know why we had to go! I don't know what anyone wanted with a schematic of the old hotel!

And, most of ALL, I don't know why my poor mother, drugged as she was, or whatever happened to her, kept talking about a child's game when I got her alone before I left. That 'hopscotch thing!'" *Jac felt as though his nerves were being fractured…with no immediate control available to him! A fleeting thought asked if he would be able to cope with the full information… should it become available to him?*

Em offered, "Maybe you didn't correctly hear your mom, or you mis-understood what she was saying. But, I know what you are saying, Jac, I didn't under-stand the "hopscotch" thing, or whatever my wife was saying, either!"

Jac nearly bellowed, "Damn it all! I'm so confused! I feel like I'm in a cheap movie! Lots of action and no substance!"

"NO, NO! It's all my fault, I shouldn't have ques-tioned your reasons for wanting to ask questions about the dumb trip we took. I'm really sorry, Jac." *Janice hoped she had covered well. It was not smart to give Jac more to 'question.' There had already been more than enough reasons to question!*

Jac was relieved hear Janice speak as though she had no ownership of clandestine information. *Even if there WAS a small niggling in the back of his brain about something he absolutely could not fathom. It just felt great to be on better terms with her. She was very special to him!*

Setting a calendar and assigning individual tasks took the better part of the evening. The three cohorts agreed to meet for breakfast. Jac and Janice walked out together, which was no surprise to Em. It truth be known, Em, very much wanted them to get married as soon as possible. His thinking was, a marriage would help settle things in the office so they could get on with earning money!

The walk to toward the car was made in silence.

Janice was the first to speak, "My apartment or yours?"

"Mine's fine. I have the most room." Jac seemed preoccupied.

Janice was certain Jac would never be the old Jac she fell in love with unless she answered all of his questions…and answered them honestly! Before Jac could open the car door, Janice drew him close to her and kissed him gently on the lips. "Jac, what say we have a good sleep and enjoy a little *'togetherness.'* I think I can do a much better job answering your questions about your mom and the old homestead if given more background on the town of Warsaw. Not so much for me personally, but to help me understand why on earth, The Supervisor sent us there. I know how he works! He's not the great Citizen for all man-kind he pretends to be!"

Jac thoughtfully responded, "I had an idea he was no great shakes when push came to shove."

"Jac, I don't know what you just said but it sounded right!"

Jac gave her a gentle nudge, "Get in before I leave you on the curb."

"That sounds horrible! Would you really leave me on the curb?"

Jac stopped for a moment, then, "Jeeze, don't you know that was just an old joke! Everybody said it to their kids! My dad always said it!" Jac smiled, "Only one time, he really left my sister and I on the road and we walked two miles to get home. He said the reason for leaving us was my stupidity in allowing anyone to burn my chest! Frankly, I didn't think he ever cared what happened to me. This time I think he was thinking about how he could make it 'pay.'"

Janice got into the car. "Jesus! What do you mean" burn your chest?"

What's that all about? And, better still...where was your mom when all this happened?"

Jac was at the rear of the car when he thought he heard her say something. "Were you talking to me? Wait 'til I get In."

"Never mind I don't think I want to hear the answer." Janice snuggled up to Jac as closely as possible. "Damn gearshift!"

Spending The Night
With Jac

The couple walked arm in arm to the door. Janice felt a growing excitement as she imagined the thrill of finally 'bedding' this beautiful man! She wondered how he would initiate sex. She refused to allow any negative thoughts. After all, this could be the beginning of a fulfilled *'for-ever-after.'*

Jac interrupted the moment by asking, "What do you want to eat? We don't want to waste too much time...we really need our rest!

Janice couldn't hold back, "Jac, in that vein, we HAVE to talk! I mean tonight! The question of, WHEN will we have the PRIVATE time you promised?

This has gone on far enough! You make me CRAZY!'

"Glad to know I have some effect on you! I promise, we will have 'the talk' and get everything straightened out! After we eat, we don't have enough here, let's go to the corner."

They walked to the corner diner, enjoyed a sandwich and soda which both knew would be followed by a lovely cabernet when they got home... *although, 'rushed… tonight.* "Jac, do we always have to walk almost a mile after every meal. I don't mind when you go off and do it alone, but why do you need company?"

"It's not for the company. I don't want us to get fat. I hate soft bodies."

"Do you mean 'dislike' or do you really mean 'hate?'"

"I mean hate! My sister has a soft body and she's young. It makes me sick to my stomach."

"Well, for what it's worth, I'm glad you told me."

"Hey! Wait a minute! I didn't mean you! You have great arms and legs; your rear is as hard as a rock!"

Janice looked shocked. In measured syllables she said, "When … have …you … ever…put a hand.. on my body?"

"The night we slept on the same bed in my first apartment."

"My, God! You felt me up while I was asleep! What kind of man are you?"

"I didn't want to upset you, we hadn't known each other very long. I just didn't want you think that all I wanted was to jump your bones. I respected you too much!"

"Trust me! I have absolutely no reason to think you want, or ever wanted to jump my bones, or anything else for that matter. Let's just say you are a 'nice-different.'"

They were passing the brick church at Third and Western when Jac seemed to come to his senses, "I think we just had your talk, Janice, and you made

yourself quite clear." My talk however, is a bit different." [*He meant 'questions' not 'sex.'*]

Jac sounded so crest fallen Janice took him by his
shoulders, turned him toward her and gently kissed
him on both eyes. That's when she tasted the salty
tears, "If you like, we can have **your** 'talk' when we
get home, Jac." *Janice felt completely in the dark.
She had no idea what Jac, specifically, wanted to talk
about. Afraid to rock the boat, she decided she would
just ride out the feelings.*

∽

No one spoke until the lights were off. Jac had insisted
they sleep in the same bed, but wanted to talk before
they fell asleep. "Janice, I know you don't really know
me. I'm not easy to 'know.' I've been a loner most of
my life except for my mom and the Navy. Both told me
what to do and when to do it! My father told me what
not to do. I'm getting my first taste of doing things on
my own. Even in Law school, I had to keep to their
schedule. Everyone in my life has had a schedule!
And, I want very much to change a few things!"

Janice sat up in bed, "You want to change...me?
Is it because I only wanted to wear the tops from your
PJs and not the bottoms"

"NO. Not that way. Don't talk silly! Janice I want
you to marry me!"

"You! What? You want me to marry YOU?"

"The way you say it sounds as if just the thought of
it makes you sick!"

"NO! You sweet, foolish, man! I want to marry you! I'm just thinking we should have sex first to see if we are compatible. I mean, after all …""

They could have heard Jac laugh in the next three apartments, "Compatible? In spite of my total lack of experience, I PROMISE, you and I will be perfect! But I think we should wait until we get married?"

"You have to be kidding me! How can you be sure 'things' will be alright?"

Jac took her hand, gently kissed it and slowly drew it down to feel his 'promise.' "With a little help from you, we will be fantastic in our marital bed!"

A very flushed Janice was barely able to respond, "I agree, Jac. How soon can we get married?"

"In a few days. We'll give our friends a little time to get the presents. I'm sure they will want to help with a few things since we are just starting out. Don't you agree? I think a small dinner party would be the place to announce our engagement. I'll bet you want the whole nine yards. Right?"

"What do you mean, 'the whole nine-yards?'" *The idea of a pre-staged dinner to get presents for the wedding left Janice with very a sour taste. Thinking she wanted a formal wedding was even more pre-posterous! Where had those ideas been generated? Probably from some kid in the Navy who knew less about etiquette than Jac.*

"Jac continued without taking a breath, "I'll bet you want a long white dress, a Bride's Maid, flowers, and a church. And, I'll wear a starched shirt and a cummerbund with my Tux. And, a High Hat, if you want! How about them apples?"

"You are joking …aren't you, Jac?"

"NO. I thought every girl wanted her wedding to be special."

"Well, this girl wants her **man** to be special. Not the wedding! And as for you in a Tux; Please, God, GIVE ME A BREAK!"

"You think I'm funny looking?"

"NO! Not FUNNY looking, you just look too serious to be a buffoon in a high hat! I fell in love with the man you see in the mirror at this moment!"

"It's dark, remember? Mind if I tissue?" Playfully, Jack attempted to steal a kiss on her lips. She hit his nose with her forehead. Jac lamented, "Please, God, help me remember to turn the lights on FIRST!"

"Are you bleeding?"

"Yes."

"Things aren't settled yet…you know."

"I know, but can I stop bleeding before we turn to…world peace?"

Janice bounded out of bed and returned with a cold, wet towel. "Here! Hold it on your nose. *What she had to say would go over better in the dark.* Now! I'm talking about us. We need to make plans for one of us moving, making a budget, and knowing what we want in one year, two years, or five years. Are you a workaholic? Do you want me to work with you? Do you want kids? Do you want vacations? Do you want to bathe in the morning or at night? Is it Okay if I hang hose over the bathtub?"

Missing her mouth in the dark, Jac gently placed his hand over her nose and forehead and said, "Enough! The answers are; you move; making money; no; yes; no, not for a long while; yes; in the morning; and it'd okay with me! There! Does that answer all your questions? Almost forgot, we can be married by a JP if you prefer."

"Fine. What about the budget?"

"Don't worry about it! We can share."

"I don't have any money!"

"I know, go to sleep!"

32. Meeting Come to Order

The Third Quarter Meeting of the Committee Brothers of the Cabal was held in the San Pedro WWII bunker where general meetings were held. Brothers were asked to come to order; with the local Supervisor being responsible for the minutes. He had just reported the successful trip to Warsaw, Illinois, led by Agent JM (Janice Marrs). And, the unexpected find of the Depot Hotel's original blue prints, complete with hidden passages and escape routes never before reported. *Something Janice had not shared with her 'office team.' As the Supervisor continued his prepared report, he allowed himself to gloat over his staggering success! They would soon have their Chosen One! His goal, while not yet shared with the assembled, was now a reality…and, NO ONE, present or absent, had neither idea nor suspicion of its achievement. He had volunteered for the 'least' of the prize assignments. Worked tirelessly on projects well beneath his station! Put-up with the weak and the ignorant! Prayed when they prayed. Gave allegiance to their goals. Chanted their Mantra at every assembly. The prize was his and he earned every single gram of it! "They search for wisdom, I will find gold!" He struggled to confine the broad smile that crept toward his lips.*

The ailing Grand Supervisor asked if there were any additions or omissions. "There being none, we ask the minutes be recorded as read." A painful coughing spasm forced the shaken man to remove himself from the room. "Will the Supervisor please continue for me?"

If fanatic zeal were a serpent, the Supervisor would have quietly slithered onto the podium. He was just where he expect to be. And, soon! He would inherit everything! "I'll be happy to continue for you, Grand Supervisor! With your permission I would like to reverse the order of our meeting by presenting some very important new business. You all need to be apprised of the FBI's current plans to use untrained personnel to protect our beloved country. While they have given all rights and authorities to this bunch, they have failed to ask the questions we believe to be the basis of our Devine heritage! Do these people believe in God? I know they don't go to Bible studies or follow any other kind of religious credo. Sad, but true, they have included into this new-formed group... one of our own. It grieves me to report she is letting us down. She questions my authority. I wouldn't be surprised if all three of them were against our God given right to carry a gun. The worst of the lot is a snot-nosed kid, fresh out of law school...who wouldn't know his tool from a hammer. His interpretation of law on some very important issues, like doing anything necessary to get the goods on our enemies, is clouding the mind of our only female member. Not that I think we should have EVER allowed a female to follow the steps of our founders! I do believe we should utilize all that God has provided us, no matter the sex. If we are going to be successful in our quest to find the Concordance of The Devine I think we had better clean our house while we can…the sooner the better. Are you with me?" *Everyone understood his words, sooner than better.*

"Supervisor, I have a question. What's the big rush, five minutes ago you were singing JM's praises? Our Agency Cabal has been looking for the Concordance for over 200 years. A few weeks shouldn't make too much difference one way or the other. I for one want to know exactly what our member, JM did that brings you to this position. Was she inappropriate with the lawyer you speak of…in less than Christian tones? And, more to the point, were you not the one who proclaimed the young Vet to be the Chosen One? Or has my memory forsaken me?"

"Excuse me for saying so, but that's just the attitude that can defeat our purpose. You need to listen and obey, Brother!" The Supervisor turned to address the remaining membership, "Anyone else have a problem? No? Good! Let's continue. I want special volunteers to work doing research of all historical evidence that might shed light on the exact Hotel location of OUR Concordance."

The Supervisor became annoyed when the question of JM's behavior was raised by several other

Brothers in attendance. Especially when "our" Concordance had been mentioned several times during the meeting."Supervisor, when did it become 'your' Concordance "What part of *follow with utmost obedience* don't you understand?"

The Little Napoleon tucked his right hand into a left-breast pocket and raised his left to signal silence. "We shall achieve our goals with or without the 'disobedient!' Our first order of business is to have me sworn in as your new Grand Supervisor, seeing as how Brother GB is unable to continue. All in favor ..."

A lone voice from the rear of the audience called out, "Suggest you hold up a minute. I'm sorry I was unable to return sooner. I've been here just long enough to hear that I am supposed to have let the group down by disobeying some rule with which I'm not acquainted. I can't imagine what I've missed, but I'm here now to answer any questions."

"The fact you interrupt these proceedings is proof enough of your obstinate behavior! Sit down and be quiet!" The Supervisor was livid.

The Grand Supervisor recognized the presence of Julie Marrs...he recovered sufficiently to stand and ask, "Supervisor, will you please be seated. I'm feeling much better. I want very much to thank you for your eager assistance ...it's much appreciated!" The old man returned to his dais.

He addressed Janice, "My Dear, You are out of breath! Won't you please come up here and say hello to your friends. I'm sure they would love to hear about

your trip to Illinois. I can't tell you how surprised I was
to learn you had been sent."

"That doesn't surprise me, Sir. I wondered why
you would want me to run the risk of jeopardizing
our objective. I freely elected to join the Brethren in
the quest for whatever is rightfully the property of the
United States. Our Supervisor's behavior leads me to
think he has developed a personal agenda. I had the
sense he wanted me to collect vital information for his
use alone. At no time did he suggest that I exchange
my findings with you or any Brother. His attitude
towards me has changed from professional superior
to lecherous male.

I very much want to have a clear understanding
with everyone. I will only remain IF the Supervisor is
no longer my superior, otherwise I leave you with my
solemn promise to retain my pledge to hold in silence
the Brotherhood and The Mission. Should you decide
my departure is appropriate, I am available to you for
Exodus. As an aside, you are the first to know of my
engagement to Jac Cartwright."

Everyone, except the Supervisor stood and
applauded. Other voices shouted, "Good for you, JM!"
"'Atta, Girl!" "Stay!" "Don't go!" "We need you!"

The Grand Supervisor stood banging his gavel,
"Brothers, Brothers, I understand your message. We
will excuse our good friend and meet in special ses-
sion. JM, this shouldn't take long. Would you step
outside for a few moments, please?"

The old building WWII bunker served the Brotherhood well. Security, and, Location. The only drawback

for someone waiting outside the actual meeting room was the lack of a place to sit. Janice paced back and forth surveying the small cross at the base of her thumb. She marveled how perfectly it nested within the normal folds of her palm. She envisioned how it would change when the last cut was made...should the cabal decide to expunge her Membership Agreement. Just as her thoughts returned to the law office, a deafening alarm sounded. Janice had to hold her nose closed and blow, in an attempt to clear her ears. She couldn't hear a thing. Turning to check with the others, a gunshot rang out just as she opened the door. What she viewed was a lifelike tableau; Brethren slouched in-place; some looked to be reaching, others ducking their heads, and while one near her lay bleeding on the floor.

୧୬

"Did Janice say where she was going this morning?"

"No, Boss. She just said she had to do something and would return in a couple of hours. Hey! Did you see how much mail we have this morning. I hope every Monday is this lucrative!

Do you think I should open it...or wait for Janice?"

"Go ahead and open it, she may not return for a while." Jac checked the fifth street window. "I wonder where she went." Jac brightened considerably! "I'll get it taken care of...enough work! Let's go to O'Kelly's and celebrate! It's not every day a Guy asks his Gal to marry him!"

"Okay. But you want to go Without Janice?"

"Well, she's not here is she? Do you have a problem with our going?"

"Well, yes! I mean after all, she put most of this
together for us, I think we need to cut her a bit of
cloth on this one. I can't even imagine how she
would feel if she came back and found we had gone
out to celebrate. I mean her feeling would really be
hurt. I doubt she would feel that you really care for
her!."

"Gee, I guess I see things differently. If it's my
money, my time, and my desire I think I have a right
to do whatever I want."A crestfallen, Em turned away
from Jac...pretending to sort mail. "I think I'll wait in
the office."

Jac busied himself with a file that was upside
down. He wondered how a person can be so happy
one minute and so frustrated the next. he wasn't really
sure what he was feeling.

He wanted to say something to Em but he thought
it would make himself appear weak. He had enough
trouble making people think his life was in control. He
wanted to learn how to measure human feelings. All
he knew was he could recognize his own feelings but
was completely lost when it came to the feelings of
others. Also strange, was the realization that sometimes his feelings felt like thoughts...surely, there
must be a formula, or something to tell the difference.
Maybe, Freud would have an answer, not that he was
any great devotee of the new thing called ' cognitive
psychology.'

"Hey, Boss I'm sorry to be a wet blanket! I should not have talked to you that way. Not when you have been so great!"

Jac flushed with embarrassment. He knew he should have been the first to speak, not his subordinate. "Em, I hope you can forgive me. At this moment, I feel a perfect ass! *Of course, being a perfect ass helps...anything to be a little better 'than.'" Since Jac was the type to replay his word, he felt even worse than before.*

"Forget it, Boss. What say we go outside, come back, and start over again?"

The phone on Jac's desk rang. "Jac Cartwright." *He listened for several minutes.* "What can I do to help?" *Another pause.* "Where are you?" *A longer pause.* "Em and I will be there in ten minutes!" Jac grabbed his briefcase. "Em, lock the door behind us!" Jac bounded down the stairs, with a much slower Em bringing up the rear, no elevator today... too slow for this mission."Where the hell, is the San Pedro Police Station?"

"Beats the hell out of me, Jac. Let's find a cop!"

Jac wanted Em to drive...ostensibly to allow himself to scan the streets for an officer. "Why do you suppose Janice is in a Police station? I doubt she did anything wrong."

Em had never heard Jac so harried. "Don't worry, Boss. Besides, start looking for a cop."

Em, for God's sakes! Stop saying 'cop,' they are police officers. Let's have a little respect!"

"Sorry. I was going to say that I know Western Avenue goes to the ocean and the City at the end is

San Pedro. I guess in the excitement I didn't have my thoughts together."

Jac felt another flush of embarrassment. "Just hang with me, Em. I'm the one, sorry! You haven't done anything to deserve my rotten behavior! I can fly a plane. Park it on a postage stamp. Lead a fly-ing squadron. But can't keep it together for a trip to a police station."

"I'm no Doc, but I'd say you have trouble when you don't have 'full control.'"

"Boy, I really am childish, aren't I?"

"Okay, Boss, enough soul-searching for one day! Let's get back to helping Janice."

⌒◯

Twenty miles and forty-minutes later the two walked into the San Pedro Police Station. The sigh above the station had seen better days. "Gee. Wouldn't you think they could have spared a little paint for the sign?"

The place was teeming with those coming in, and those trying to get out, a sundry assortment of attor-neys trying to bail clients, three ladies of the night striking suggestive poses near a back wall, and one lone Desk Officer of the Day trying to manage the hoard.

"I don't see Janice. Let's wait a minute to see if things slow a bit."

"Jac, aren't you the one who said, 'the squeaking wheel gets the grease?'"

"Right!" Jac muscled his way to the desk. "I'm here to speak with Janice Marrs."

The Desk Sergeant immediately, rose from his seat and motioned for Jac to follow. Down a short, well worn, hallway Jac was ushered into a closet of a room. Only large enough for a chair and a single person sitting down.

Janice stood and threw her arms around Jac. "You will never know how happy I am to see you!"

Jac ignored Janice. He removed her arms. "Sergeant, is there any reason Miss Marrs can't leave?"

"I would say, a pretty good one. She's being held for murder."

Jac felt the blood drain from his head and arms. "I see. Is there a room where I can speak to my client?"

"I don't think so. We are waiting for the FBI. It seems she has some friends in high places...not that it will do much good here. Chief Goodwin hates high-mucky-mucks! You've seen her, you can wait outside or you can come back tomorrow."

Janice looked like some unseen jolt had just destroyed her underpinnings...both men caught her as she fainted. She wasn't known to have any medical problem, but she remained unconscious long enough to be moved to a larger room.

Jac cuddled her like a baby. He kept repeating, "Come on, wake up, wake up."

Weakened, she whispered, "Can you help me?"

"The truth is, I don't know. I don't even know what happened. Do you want to tell me?"

Janice didn't have the opportunity to answer. The FBI arrived. "The FBI is here and they don't need help. You can leave."

Jac found Em a block from the station. "I saw Janice. She's being held for murder! The FBI just came."

Em could not help thinking Jac's demeanor could be identified as one belonging to a radio news-caster. Informative, dry, devoid of feeling. "My, God, Jac! You sound like you're reading from a paper! How is she? Is she hurt? Who said she murdered someone? Aren't you going to help her?"

"I'm not a criminal attorney," was Jac's only response.

"Fine! Do we eat? Do I call my wife to come and get me? Do we stay to be with her...what?"

"Do whatever you like. I need to take a rest in the car." Jac began walking back toward the station. *Why did this have to happen to me...now? Everything was going great! I was doing better when I didn't have to worry about anyone else. Now I'm not sure what I want. A good nap should help..*

Em lost his appetite. Jac's attitude took Em to an emotional state he preferred not to engage. Who was this man who had offered so much to Janice and me? And, now acts like a stranger. Was this really going to be the end of the fearless-three? Or, was there something he could do?

By the time he reached the car Jac was sound asleep, he decided to take the 'reins' and run with them! "Wake up, Sleeping Beauty! We have things to do and people to see!" Shaking Jac vigorously, "Get your lazy butt off the seat and make plans so we can rescue our fair-damsel!"

Jac was always easy to rouse, thank the Navy for that. "All right, all right! I'm awake!" Jac sat up, stretched his arms and announced, "Good on you, My Friend! Old Doc used to say that. So, what's on our docket?"

"We both go in there and demand to see Janice! We refuse to leave her side! Even if they put both of us in jail!"

Jac was forced to manage a weak laugh, "Don't you think that's going a bit too far?"

"Not on your tin-type! We do it and we do it now."

"Okay, whatever you say. I'm too tired to lead right now."

The crowd in the station had thinned some. Em was able to signal the sergeant for directions to the men's room.

When Em took Jac's arm Jac complained, "I don't have to 'go.'"

"So. What? Do you know a better way to find Janice? We'll just open doors until we find her! *Em couldn't help thinking,' the man has gone over the edge. he's acting like a real fruitcake, is he danger-ous?'*

The stench from the men's room brought Jac into the moment. "God, that smells! Let's find Janice!"

"Glad to have you back, Boss! Give me some warning when you decide to do that again! I was beginning to think you were gone for good."

"We can talk about it later." *It seemed to Jac that he was always saying,'we'll talk about it later'. And, 'later' never seems to come…'always too tired', 'not enough time', 'it's late,' or more promising, perhaps 'later.'*

Em read the Direction Board hanging on a chair. "It seems we might get lucky if we check both interrogation rooms. You need to do the talking."

"Whatever you say. True, I do have more clout!" *There was the big 'I' again!* "Damn, I hate when I do that!"

"Do what? What are you talking about?" Just a slight push and Em had found Janice and Agent Croft on one side of a table and three officers on the other. With a broad smile, Em offered, "Here we are…all in our places."

"Enough with the nursery rhymes! We have a murder on our hands! And, who the HELL are you?"

"Happy to meet you, Chief Goodwin. I'm Jac Cartwright, attorney… not criminal, just insurance; and a good friend of Miss Marrs."

Janice spoke for the first time since she had been ushered into the room, "Gee, and here I thought we were engaged?"

The intent of her words was not lost on Jac, he just felt too unsure of everything and everyone…at the moment.

"Good enough! I like you, Youngman! You are not one of those hair-slick-back, smart-ass kids from LA. Both of you have a seat and we'll try to straighten this thing out." He turned to Agent Croft, "Why is the FBI interested in this young lady."

"It's simple, Chief. She is one of our Agents, as are both Mr. Cartwright and Mr. Emmery whom you have yet to meet."

"Now, If that don't beat all! You three sound too nice to be FBI!" The Chief took his pen to paper and began to record the interviews. He began with the responding officers. Next, he questioned Janice with a father-like manner. The Chief allowed Agent Croft to dictate a routine FBI response. And last, a two sentence record of Jac's lack of knowledge of the murder. "Well, folks, I'm satisfied we got all the facts we need. Youngman, you can take your little lady with you. I'll let you know when we need you."

Perfunctory 'goodbyes' behind them, the four left the station. Croft said he would contact them later. The three remained wordless until they reached Ollie Hammond's. Jac was the first to speak, "Well, Friends, I don't know if I should cross the street and get the Rabbi or go to the next corner and get the Priest."

Em broke in, "They are such good friends you'll probably will find both at the same place! Rabbi Magnin usually goes to the Good Father...St. Basil has more food."

Jac's mind was racing! Doing his best to stay in the moment, he offered, "Em is a champ at helping in tight situations! I'm not ashamed to say, were it not for him this afternoon I would have lost myself respect and a best friend! I want to apologize to all, and promise to find the secret to the thing called 'feelings.' I still feel a bit divested of a personal-self." Jac raised both hands towards his friends," Thank you for your patience. God will'in and the Cricks don't rise…we'll be fine!"

Em smiled, "Glad you know we care, Jac. But, please, enough with the down-home stuff. We've had enough for a coon age! The important thing right now is to help Janice with her sticky-wicket. There are no charges as yet, and probably won't be any later, however she will need your help. Unless this is identified as an FBI issue they will be unable to help. I'm certain you both understand."

Both nodded in agreement. "Janice, I know Jac wants to help you, but you're going to have to come clean on a few things!"

They pulled into Ollie's parking lot. A dispirited Janice asked, "Can't this wait until we get home?

"No Way, No How! Em has a right to hear everything! If the two of you think inside is not a good place to have this talk, we can sit in the car…after we eat! I'm hungry."

Em made a move to get out the car, "Glad you can eat! I'm going get a cab and go home! Janice, want to come with me?"

Jac was incredulous, "All I did was speak the truth!" *Understanding other people's sense of acceptable behavior was not in Jac's repertoire; for Jac, this was just another one of those 'no harm, no foul' situations.*

Jac's voice belied the tumult of emotions that overpowered him in the moment! His mind was racing with relationship questions, a sense of some personal responsibility for 'today', and the gut-level recognition he had no similar experience from which to find resolution. "I need to think about us, the office, the FBI, and what I do next."

"What happened to 'we'? You mean, now it's all just 'you?'"Em was about to continued when he saw Jac's sudden tears. Embarrassed beyond words, Em gently offered, "Hey, Pal, why don't we have a group hug and have breakfast...for supper; like none of this happened?"

"Do you really think that's possible?"

Janice quietly spoke for herself and Em, "We are the 'invincible three' aren't we? I don't know about the two of you fellows, but this is the worst day of my life! I'm scared nearly to death about the shooting, and afraid of losing my new little family!"

Jac wiped his tears. He was aware 'anger' and 'suspicion' were slowly losing their grip on him. A bit slack-jawed, he reached across Em and squeezed Janice's shoulder... just as he had during 'good times,' "Hey, isn't it a good thing this is a nice wide front seat!"

Em brightened, "You BET! Otherwise, I would have thought you were getting fresh!"

The three friends gave as much a 'hug' as the seat would allow, and agreed to start over.

❧

33. The Titan Bunker Investigation

The San Pedro Police Department (a Los Angeles sub-station) assigned their best forensic team to investigate the killing at the local Cabal meeting. The organization was well known to law enforcement. An Area Religions' dossier compiled recently by the Los Angeles Police Department held a extensive history of Cabal activities over some 150+ years. Never seen as a threat to the United States Government, always, seemingly, available in times of disaster and civil disobedience...and, rare to openly proselytize for personal gain. Their Mission Statement 'appeared' to be dedicated to the preservation of National History and Treasures; teaching the road to Salvation to all who even looked like they were interested. At present, or historically, no member except Janice Marrs was known to have had a Want or Warrant against them.

The Coffee Shopee next to the Pedro Station was empty when the two investigators entered. As usual, free coffee and donuts awaited them at their favorite booth. Favorite, because it was next to the Men's Room and unseen from the front window.

Flopping a well-warn pocket, notebook down on the table, Officer Raddich, (Rad to his Friends) breathed a heavy sigh, "God! I hate these cases that seem open and shut…then kick you in the family jewels! What's your take on the Marrs babe? How can she be Cabal AND FBI?"

Dwarkin, (Rad's four-year partner) opined as how, "Beats the shit out of me, man! There's no accounting for a mix of faith and fun!"

"Jesus, where did you get such a notion? Aren't you the guy that said 'women should stay in the kitchen, barefoot and pregnant? Or, was that meant only for the bow-legged ones?'"

"Yah, but did you take a look at her gams? Those didn't grow on no 'Bible Tree' if you know what I mean!"

"I sort'a felt for her. That attorney, supposed to be a friend, was a real wimp! Say you not so?"

"Yeh, you've got that right! What she needs is a real man! Hum-m-m, I wonder what the odds might be?"

"Get a grip! Let's get our prelim completed so we can get this 'ass-biter' on the road. The lab boys said we would have their information in 48 hours."

"Okay by me. Chief said to do some investigating near the downtown address. I haven't seen Wilshire boulevard in a coons age!"

"I can taste the steak right now!" Be a good Guy and drive, I need to combine our reports!"

"Sure. But you didn't say which restaurant. There's a million of them in the area."

"Musso Franks! Who else?"

"Hey, Dork ...."

"Rad! How many times have I told you...I DON'T HAVE A NICKNAME?"

"Sorry. I was going to say, it's not 'Musso Franks,' it's Musso and Franks, or something like that."

"Enough all ready! So, who gives a shit?"

"Rad, Let's hit it... LA's forty-five minutes from here!"

૭◡౨

The partners had just agreed to begin their surveillance ...when they spotted Jac's license on Wilshire Boulevard.

"Couldn't be better! I love Ollie Hammond's! I could use a good breakfast for dinner!"

"Rad, the day or time you aren't hungry, is the day I call a hearse! I do admit, I could go for some real food for a change. I'm glad the three of them don't know us. That means 'we do it in the open...for a change'"

"Dwarkin, that's the only way I like to do anything... in the open!"

"Is sex the only thing that moves you? I've known you four years, I think your wife is great and I know she loves you...I admit I don't know why. You've got a great house and drive a new car. Come to think of it, you are such a schmuck at times."

"You know you love me. I've saved your ass more than once, but who's counting?"

"Start counting, brother. I think I'm up on you by six saves. If memory serves."

"Enough! Let's go in and earn some gelt!"

"Good, there's a booth open next to our 'perps.'"

Wasting no time, the partners began sharing information in whispered tones.

"Okay, this is what I got: Monday 1:30 PM:

Thirty-four on-lookers were milling around the area approximately three hundred yards west of Harbor Boulevard, near Toumey Road (a temporary drive-through for oil trucks) leading to the deserted (?) WWII Bunker ...some twenty-five feet below ground; well hidden by heavy over-growth and sand.

"Dwarkin, that's why we work so well together! You get the stats and I get the schmaltz! Okay... next?"

"Statement and Ids were taken. Rusted locks on heavy iron doors allowed easy access. No telephones (reported shooter unknown)

"One of the two major areas within the bunker held some fifty chairs, a dais, a microphone, black board, chalk, working-clock, and electric lighting. I drew a chalk outline around the body: male, short dark hair, aprox' five feet tall, 160 to 170 pounds, age: bet 40 to 50; gun-shot to left temporal lobe, no additional identifying marks visible; white shirt, black string tie; black jacket under left hand; black pants, no belt; and no jewelry"

Rad looked up at Dwarkin, "I wrote *'see who is paying electric bill,'* since has been closed for years."

Dwarkin tapped his pen on the table, then suddenly looked up, "Did you say there was no jewelry on the man? Because if that be so, I wonder why five or six of the responding members asked to keep the Brother's necklace? They were so sure we would find one under his shirt. What do you make of that?"

"Beats me! And, no…there was no jewelry of any kind! I suppose, now they are going to say, we took it!"

"Rad, I hope the lab finishes in a hurry.

The partners had just opened their menus when… from their blindside, a arm shot beyond them, grabbed Janice by the hair, yanking her full-body out of the booth! A man nattily dressed in a grey, velvet, Prince Albert cut-away coat and trousers, with top hat and walking cane in-hand began screaming, "You owe ME! I'm your Supervisor, you BITCH!"

Wimp no more! Jac roared out of the booth, "Janice belongs to me, not you! You Son-of-a-Bitch! I'm going to choke the liven-life out of you! You, Bastard! You Cock-Sucker!

The San Pedro team sat speechless! They would have loved to have intervened; common sense prevailed. They would make notes and wait to witness what was sure to have…a 'grand' finale. The pugilists exchanged a couple of blows before the local LA Police arrived.

Information was being exchanged when one of the cops said, Hey! Is that you, Dwarkin? Shit, I haven't seen you in a coon's age! How are things in Pedro?"

A chagrinned Dwarkin slid further into the corner of the booth, hoping to be out of Jac's line of sight and said nothing in reply. He could only think, *"Some undercover cops we turned out to be!"*

The questioner bent forward, and in a stage-whisper asked, "What the hell's the matter, are you on a stakeout or something?"

The two Pedro cops nodded in unison.

"Gotcha!" In a normal voice, "Sorry man, You look just like a guy I used to be in school with. If you don't mind I'd like to know what the two of you saw and heard. Looks to me like the tall drink-of-water got in some good licks. Tell my partner what happened while I try do some sorting-out."

The Pedro team was able to finish eating just about the time the Supervisor was being handcuffed. Protesting all the while about being 'in the FBI!' No one offered to help.

"Don't worry, fella, we'll get this all sorted out at the station. Just cool down, it will only take a couple of minutes to get where we 're going."

"I'll have your badges, YOU IDIOTS! I'm an FBI Supervisor!"

"Sure you are, Fella.

∽

Janice and Em have been waiting in the Emergency Waiting about three hours. The hospital smells! Screaming patients! Emergency doors opening and closing! Medical staff yelling instructions! Emergency firemen, City and private ambulances *hurriedly* lightening their loads and leaving. Finally an EXIT door opens.

"Hi, Gang!" A pale *kid*, with a half-smile and a slack jaw tried t o sit down between the two of them…more fall than sit.

Janice was the first to speak, "Jac, what did you do to yourself? What did you break?"

"Give the poor Guy a chance, he's as white as a sheet!" Taking Jac's hand, "Here, Pal, have a seat. You poor, poor Guy!" Em took Jac's elbow, "Is your arm broken?"

"No…just my wrist and hand I think. But, I'm NOT sorry!" Jac took Janice's hand, "Do you love me? I need to know! If you do, I want the three of us to (*raising his voice to a deafening range*) FORGET EVERYTHING THAT HAS HAPPENED IN THE LAST THIRTY HOURS AND START OVER!"

"Okay. It's okay, Jac! You don't have to yell, we understand." Em encouraged Jac to walk toward the car. "Do you need a wheelchair?"

"Hell, no! Janice give me your hand!" Jac got into the car without waiting for Janice.

"Jac, you frighten me! What's happened to you? I do want to be with you, but …" *Janice reasoned it must be the pain medication having something of a paradoxical reaction.*

"There are NO BUTS! I'm just doing what I should have done years ago! I'm taking control!" He saw Janice wince, "NO, I didn't mean you. I mean control of myself! No more making nice! No more 'sorry,'…

'of course, whatever you say' … 'whatever you want,' just…NO MORE!"

Em questioned, "What about our talk? Is it still on?"

Jac slumped deeper into the upholstered seat, "Guys, I'm really tir…"

Janice kissed his forehead, "Bless him! He's exhausted. I think everything is going to be fine." She turned to Em who was preparing to drive, "Take us to his apartment, I'll stay the night and you can come by in the morning so we can have a verbal catharsis."

∽

The San Pedro Investigation Team, preparing to leave the hospital, smiled at the irony.

Rad, spoke, "The poor Guy, finds a 'voice' and it costs him a broken arm and wrist. "Do you think we should we report the altercation? We were able to do the emergency requirements, and the ' Supervisor' had it coming! What do you think?"

"Considering the Bastard's ID had him as FBI, I would DO nothing! Besides, the kid became a man tonight! I say, "Good For Him!"

"Agreed! But what do you think about the FBI Supervisor being at the Cabal and the shooting; at least that is what I was told by one of the witnesses. He said the Supervisor was some kind of Leader. Who knows?"

It's a mess! But it's getting interesting!" Raddich folded his notebook. He and his partner neared the hospital parking lot.

"Dwarkin, where did you say the It Club is located?"

"Why? Got an itch to make a change?"

"NO! It was one of the references the Supervisor gave."

"YOU HAVE TO BE KIDDING! It's a Gay Club. My God, what is the FBI coming to?"

"What's so strange, Rad? You know what they say about J. Edge, don't you?"

"Yah! This is REALLY getting interesting!"

૭⌒૭

34. Mystery Deepens

The next morning no one ate much breakfast. The three cohorts remained silent as they crossed Fifth Street. The day was as grey as the mood surrounding them.

"Hey, Gang! I know I'm just the bookkeeper slash investigator, but I would appreciate it if the two of you smiled just once before we go into our office."

"As usual, the man makes good sense. I am ready to 'set the standard' as we used to say. Here goes!" Jac managed a comedic example of a smile that made Em and Janice cough, sputter and spit...unexpectedly!"

"I didn't know I was that good!"

The three enjoyed a major, group hug...in front of everyone! "Hey! Watch the hand!"

∽

The heat was on in the office, making it a cozy place to have their talk. Janice made coffee and Jac arranged the chairs while Em opened the mail for checks.

"Sorry, No Dough, No Go!"

"What do you mean…no go?"

Em had a 'got you again, Boss' grin, "No-go-to-bank!"

"Oh, Boy. Is this what I have to look forward to… joke a minute?"

"Maybe, no…but you could use a few. Come the think of it, the promise of a corny joke could keep you on the straight and narrow. Example, no smile, one joke. What do you say?"

"Sure! I'll do anything to save myself!"

Janice sat, crossed her legs, and leaned on the desk. "Okay, Dear Friends, I'm ready! Where would you like me to start?"

"I think Em and I would like to know 'last things, first!' Meaning, What were you doing in the Bunker?"

"Well, the abandoned Bunker has been used for our general meetings for over a year. When I say 'Our,' I mean the Cabal of The Devine. It is sort of a religious organization that splintered from the International Bible Students in 1933. One if its major missions is to help in any way possible to preserve all our National History. They seem to enjoy researching old papers."

Jac interrupted, "What about Division of Church and State?"

"Well, that's what interested me. I'm a die-hard patriot! I love my country! My early experience with religion was a torrent of 'don't do this,' 'don't do that,' 'God's watching,' 'saluting a flag is the same as saluting the devil'…ad infinitum! My mother said she was 'looking for salvation!' She sure had a strange way of going on the quest. I stopped counting when she had alternately 'joined' thirty-three different, churches and cults. Believe me, it was no picnic! Anyway, getting back to the Cabal. The FBI Supervisor was the one who contacted me. I had just enrolled in LA City College when I was chosen to speak to a community group about Community Safety. It seems the school liked a paper I had written about the National Red Cross. The Supervisor was in the audience, and spoke with me after the meeting. I was, of course, flattered.

Janice continued, "Imagine, the FBI was interested in me, a twenty-five year old, from a whistle-stop in Kansas! I agreed to accept membership in the Cabal. Little did I know, the Supervisor had been a member for enough years to get himself elected to a position, just below Grand Supervisor. He explained his membership as necessary to prove loyalty...promising them protection from FBI persecution. Originally, he worked to obtain membership because the FBI assigned him to Cult Investigation. I guess some worried that the USA might inadvertently, foster a strong subversive group and end up like Germany. He regaled me with stories of his counter-spy prowess. He boasted he had, single-handedly, averted a confrontation with a 'fallen-away' group of Cabal-ites. I learned later he did nothing more than make a phone call to the other folks and threaten to 'sic' the FBI on them. Apparently, he used the same pitch on me that they used on him...'help us preserve our Nation's History.' As you can see, it worked equally well on me.

Anything for my Country! His Membership Reports to the FBI must have been stellar. He continued to rise in the ranks of the FBI, as well as the Cabal. As an aside, you might be interested in the fact that I am the only female ever allowed into their Senior Ranks. That fact was just another (flattery), 'feather' in my proverbial cap! A big head, or WHAT? I'm learning my lesson, though. The Supervisor and I simultaneously learned the possible location of the twelve, golden spikes... representations of the Twelve Apostles. You might know them as the twelve, missing, Golden Spikes from the 1869 Celebration of The Golden Spike?" Janice looked for an sign of recollection by either Em or Jac.

Jac raised his hand, "What do you mean... twelve golden spikes? I thought there was only one. The one driven into a rail at Promontory Point, Utah."

"Oh, I thought it was common knowledge there were thirteen gold spikes forged for a David Hewes, who gave one spike to Governor Stanford for the celebration, which was removed. The Governor gave it back to Hewes after the ceremony. Hewes, in-turn, gave it to the Stanford Museum. Anyway, the main point is, twelve, golden spikes went missing. These were believed to be in a National Treasures Vault. About six months ago, the vault was opened... no spikes!"

"My God! What happened? The things must have weighed a ton."

"Not quite, Em. Each had a gold weigh of only fourteen point-three troy ounces."Jac thought for a moment, "But how much total weight for each? There must have been a base of something; Pot metal, steel,...something!"

"It's not the weight...it's the worth." Jac, you're always the worry-wart!"

"Good thing he is...he's our protector, remember?"

Janice gave Jac's hand a soft pat, his only response was a weak smile. "As for the gold content...seventeen point-six carats of gold alloyed to copper. But Guys, their real value is NOT the gold! There's a rumor the remaining twelve spikes are fashioned in the features of the Apostles. That's the value! The Vatican has offered one billion dollars! Collectors are willing to pay more. That's why the Supervisor is rabid on the subject of finding them...willing to take any risk necessary!"

"If the Supervisor is working outside the confines of the FBI, why has he been allowed to persist?" The furrow in Jac brow was deepening.

"Is the son-of-a-bitch a master at hoodwinking, or are most FBI folks simple minded...easily duped?"

"That's a little sharp, don't you think? You sound a little like the Supervisor. You sound like 'you're better than!'" *Janice bit her lip. She could have said more but elected not to rock the boat more than she already had.*

"Thanks for the compliment!"

Em could not hold back, "Damn it! Will the two of you just shut up and listen for a minute!" Turning toward Jac and looking him full in the face, "We came into this office full of promise this morning! We were ready to start over! To regain our love for each other!

219

What happened? Well, I'll tell you! Jac, you sound like an egotistical prick when you demean others! Especially, Janice! Is that who you are? OR…are you just a jealous fool who hasn't the balls to speak from his heart because he can't share 'control?' That's damn stupid in my book! Okay, I quit! No more talk from me!"

Jac started to stand, but dropped down hard on his seat. "I've just looked into a mental mirror, again and what I saw frightens me. Why does it take twenty-nine years to begin maturation?"

Em smiled, "Sorry, can't help you; 'better late than never' maybe?"

Jac couldn't help laughing, "God, I really love you, man! Speak anytime you like."

"What about 'US'? Do we continue as a group of three or should I finish our talk first, so you can determine how you feel about me?" *Janice had never looked so uncomfortable.*

Jac moved his chair a bit closer to Janice and took her hand, "There's only ONE reason we want you to continue…we're flabbergasted by your revelations! This is better than the *Molle Mystery Theater* on radio!"

Janice ignored Jac's, attempt to 'make light,' "Okay. Before I continue, don't you think it might have been more than coincidence that brought the three of us together; in what seemed like a flash? The Supervisor was given a plum of an assignment that gave him an introduction to different levels of LA society. Plus, he had the sanctity of a strong government that gave a level of latitude... few citizens have. He is a smooth manipulator. Even the two of you fell for his sudden departure from Croft's plan. And, where did we go? We had to go to Jac's home town... interesting, huh? And, why did I have to go to the Depot Hotel?"

"That's a very good question, Janice. Why were we sent to my home town?"

"Simple! The Cabal members had embarked on an extensive research that pointed to Warsaw, Illinois as the possible location of the spikes. More directly... the Depot Hotel!"

Jac collapsed his body as he sank in his chair, lifting his head a bit, "I can't believe this! Where did they get their information?"

"I forgot to mention the Cabal of The Devine has some six million members in the United States alone. About fifty million in the world. Someone or something must have led them to Warsaw."

"Are they bigger than the Catholics?" Em asked, furrowed brow and wide-eyed.

"I don't know, but more than half of them call themselves Christians; According to the Supervisor. I don't know anything else about them. Just what he's told me."

Jac sat shaking his head and looked at Janice, "Nothing makes any sense! I get a job, NO, first I meet you. Then, I get a job. I meet Em. I lose a job, but that leads to Croft and the FBI! Now, the two of you agree to work with me, and we get an office! We join the FBI, ostensibly to provide information for the Jap problem, but an FBI Supervisor sends us to Illinois for some gold spikes! And, we haven't even gotten to the murder yet. So, Janice! Where in the hell are we in this mess?"

"I don't know!"

"Well, did you know the women who was shot?"

"What woman? There are NO women, other than myself!"

"Sorry! It's just that one of the cops told me she was about forty and looked like a man in her tailored suit and silk tie. He said he had to laugh when he opened his..er..her shirt and got hit in the face with a perfect, well-developed rack and a great pair of nice wide hip bones!"

"You have to be kidding! Where was she hit? No one told me anything!. All I know... the police grabbed me by the arms and forced me into the patrol car, then CUFFED me to an arm rail. No one spoke to me until you came to the station."

"Well, all they told me was that it was a weird shot; hit the femoral artery in the groin and she bled to death in short time. The gun was identified by some-one in the bunker who said it was yours, and that guns were never allowed in any proximity to Bunker, by any member, no matter *rank*. Do you have any idea why they would say it was yours?"

"Sure do! Because it was mine! I had no idea any-one had been able to take it from my belt holster. The Supervisor was the only one who knew I had the gun. In fact, he made me 'carry' since we left for Illinois."

Janice winced, "My God, do you think he was the one who identified the gun?"

Jac's only answer, "THAT SON-OF-A-BITCH!"

Em whistled between two fingers, "Jesus! Jac, get a grip! So, what do you think? Do the cops think Janice is in the care of the FBI right now? Is she AWOL or something? We don't need any more trouble than we have at the moment."

"Get a grip YOURSELF! Do you really think I would go out of my way to start a cataclysm; there are only three of us and a ton of them! Get REAL! She is out on her own recognizance because of her FBI guarantors." Jac turned toward Janice, "I want to be the ONLY one responsible for protecting you! No FBI! No Outsider! Just me! I love you! I promise to do whatever it takes to keep you free from ANY harm! I'm nothing like my dad! I respect women; this one I love!" His hug was huge.

"Okay, Boss, I get the message, but you know how things can turn...when you least expect it!"

Jac wasn't sure how to answer Em. All he could muster was, "Don't end your sentences with a preposition!"

Equal exchanges of reassurance for Janice's safety, and promises of a full and prosperous future as Cartwright and Associates, the Three were back on track!

Janice was the one to suggest that she be allowed to complete 'her story.' She carefully detailed every assignment she had been given by the FBI Supervisor. Especially, those having to do with Jac. Explaining how, all the while, the Supervisor did

everything FBI propriety would allow to get her to
bed. Her rebuffs only heightened his cunning. He had
purposefully, sent her on assignments that could have
ruined any opportunity she might have for a normal
future, bordering on the possibility of incarceration.
She explained her involvement had become so deep
she had no viable out. At least, none that she could
think of, considering her unrelenting fear of the name-
less, possible consequences.

Jac and Em remained silent. Neither moved.

"Well, does this silence mean you both want me
gone?"

Jac put his arms around her.

Em added an arm, "God, Janice, you're like the kid
sister I never had, just smarter than she would have
been."

No one was listening. Jac lifted Janice's chin, "I
told you…I LOVE YOU! I have a wizard idea! It's been
a very, long afternoon. All of us are tired. Let's have
a great, early supper and get a better night's rest
tonight! What do you say?"

"Speaking for Janice and myself, I would say that
really is a wizard idea!"

Janice was consumed with fear of reprisal. The
Supervisor had the power to cause bad things to happen while she was still being considered as a murder
suspect. *There would not be thoughts of love or sex
this night! Sleep would have to provide the much
needed respite from all things fearsome.*

∽

35. Jac Has A Dream

The door to Jac's second bedroom opened, a yawning Janice bent down, kissed Jac on the mouth and asked, "Going to sleep all day?"

Still sleepy, Jac pulled her close, "Sit down for a minute, Lady!" Rubbing his eyes, "Boy, do I have a story to tell you!"

"Sounds terrific! Can I crawl-in with you while you tell me?"

"Not now, I don't want to forget any of the details."

Janice gently punched Jac in the ribs, "Should I take notes."

"Hey! Stop it! I'm being serious!"

"So am I!" She tickle-punched him harder this time.

"I had the dream to end all dreams! You agreed to marry me ...on the spot!"

"You're kidding? Right?"

"No, I am not! In the dream, Em thought it was a great idea and got Rabbi Magnin from the Wilshire Temple to marry us! He even let us borrow a ring the Catholic Priest next door gave him for his birthday. The Rabbi was great! It was the kind of wedding you said you wanted! You would have loved it! One of these days I'm going to research his religion. He said

225

it was based on the concept of Love and love alone. Sounds nice to me. But! Then the important part of the dream happened."

Janice smiled, "More important than our getting married?"

"No! You know what I mean. Important to our future. I got to 'see' my behavior…my real behavior. To explain, let me share how I grew up…how people acted towards other people. My dad never showed any respect for my mother. I think I mentioned that before. Well, I was told it didn't matter how you say things, only what you say. So, can you see there was no room for 'how a man might feel' when he spoke to others? Janice, I could cry when I think of the hurtful things I have said to you. It's a good thing Em was around to point those out to me. In fact, in the dream he really read the riot act to me, what "I want", where "I want to go," he just went on and on and on! Well, trust me, things are going to change!" So, what do you think of my dream?"

"That was no dream, Sweetheart, that was worse than a nightmare! How do you feel"

"I feel TERRIFIC! Best I've felt in YEARS!" Jac kissed Janice, "CASE CLOSED!"

Em was waiting for them in the restaurant. "I hope the two of you feel as great as I do this morning."

"This is one of the best mornings I've ever had! Jac had what I believe was a liberating dream. It sounded like he was given an opportunity to evaluate some personal material."

"Janice is right! That's exactly what happened! I've been a good example of a country hick!

Not that all who live a country life are as out of it I've have been. I admit I have much to learn, but I feel I'm going to make greater strides in a shorter time. It's just those damn old notions of how things are supposed to be accomplished. At home you learned that it's not how you say words but what words you say. Feeling don't count! But now I know better!" He gave Janice a soft kiss.

৩৩

The Invincible Three enjoyed their usual breakfast. Sated! Faced a new day in their office.

"I check the mail for money, Jac."

"Thanks, Em. Janice and I wi.." The phone rang.

Janice answered, "Cartwright and associates, how may I assist you?" Janice listened quietly, "I'll be happy to assist. Will one hour fit your schedule? I think it will take us some forty-five minutes to get to San Pedro."

"What did they want?" Jac sounded worried. "Should I get Terry to represent you? I don't want you to be placed in any jeopardy."

"From what was said, I doubt I'll have any trouble. I was wishing that was Croft on the phone …I may need his help. I'm hoping the three of us can go together."

৩৩

36. Case Closed: Mystery Solved

The police gym was selected for the meeting. Larger, quieter, and more chairs. The Captain handed Janice a list of questions to look over. "Do as much research as necessary to complete my Case Closed Report. "Take as much time as you need. I won't be looking for your report before the middle of next week. However, these are a couple of things I'm curious about." He placed a check mark by each on the list."

Jac was stunned hearing Janice had been 'cleared' of all charges without even a phone interrogation. "It sounds as though you have apprehended your perpetrator. May we be privy to the information? Or are 'the powers that be' wanting to maintain an anonymity?"

"Yes. No. And, yes. Sorry about that, but that's the way it has to be, at least for now."

Jac felt completely disrespected. "Of course! I understand! I was just expecting a bit of professional courtesy." No one paid attention to his words.

Janice examined the list. "I think I might be able to recall the answer to number twelve by memory, or would you prefer I type out the information for your file?"

"Typed would be fantastic! But I'm damn curious to have an idea what it's like."

"Okay. I'll do my best, here goes. The Cabal of The Devine Mantra starts out 'Lord hear our prayer', Honor to thee each day of our life. 'Lord hear our prayer,' Obedience is the path to life everlasting, 'Lord hear our prayer,' Prayer lights the way to salvation, 'Lord hear our prayer,' Sup.."

The Captain interrupted Janice, "I think I get it! Does the beginning letter of each entreaty have significance?"

"Yes. It ultimately spells HOPSCOTCH."

"That's what I thought!"

Jac sucked in his breath. His hands began to shake. Doc Harks, Em's wife, and the necklace that hung from his neck. A very pale Jac asked, "I think I'm involved in some way. I'm not at all sure... how. Who is really in charge of this investigation. I can't believe the FBI would allow a police department to do more than gather information."

"Well, isn't that what I said earlier?"

"You for sure didn't mention the FBI." Jac was still bristling from a previously *assumed* insult."

Janice was checking her list again, "I see you want to know how often the group met. Well, I was only aware of a monthly meeting. The FBI Supervisor said It wasn't necessary for me to attend unless he called me first."

"Whoa! Wait a darn MINUTE! What do you mean... the FBI Supervisor?"

"Just what I said! The FBI Supervisor gave me the original assignment to attend certain meetings in order to glean information about some research the International Cabals were doing." Janice thought for a moment, "What's the problem? You folks have him in custody downtown because of a fight he had with Mister Cartwright."

The Captain began to rise from his chair, "You're telling me...we...have him... downtown...on a misdemeanor charge? God! I don't understand any of this! I'll be back in a minute."

Em had been so quiet he was completely overlooked by both Janice and Jac. "Em, I'm so sorry! Pull your chair next to us, what did you think when you heard about the 'hopscotch' thing. I remembered your own wife had a stranger visit with a hopscotch necklace."

"I was just as shocked as you looked, Jac. What do you make of all of this?"

"I don't have a clue! I guess we will have to depend on Janice for further light on the subject. It's too convoluted for me!" He gave Janice a warm kiss.

"If that means 'flummoxed' than I'm with you... all the way!" Em turned toward Janice, "What's the kicker? I do much better if I have an idea what a problem looks or smells like. Is something supposed to happen to us; and when will it happen?"

"Em, so help me God, I don't know! I'm in as much of the dark as you are! And, that's the truth!"

Jac put his arms around Janice, "How about a kiss to make all of us feel a little more like a united front?"

The Police Captain re-entered the room, "What kind of religion is Cabal of The Devine? Is it Catholic or, is it plain old Christian?"

Janice assumed the question was for her, "I don't have a clue. Why do you ask? Is it important?"

"Beats me! But I just learned the Masonic Judge wanted the Supervisor to go free, but the Catholic Judge is holding him." The Captain added, "The poor guy is caught in the middle of a political stand-off."

Jac quickly interjected, "Don't feel too sorry for him! He has many irons in fires few know anything about. I wouldn't be a bit surprised if, by the time everything 'shakes out,' you will have found an international connection. Janice, didn't you say the Cabal, originally broke from some International Bible Students organization? That would make sense why the Catholic wants him held. I'm no religious scholar, but when religious groups 'break from' isn't it usually 'from' the Catholics? And, what about the gold?"

The Captain turned towards the door, sputtering like a leaky gasket, "WHAT... GOLD? What the hell are you talking about?"

Jac was quick to respond, "Ask the Supervisor when you get to him. He knows all about the gold spikes!"

"This is too much for me!" He turned toward Janice, "Give me a moment and I'll have a Release From Hold for you."

The ubiquitous Em needed to have the last word... "THAT was easy!"

❧

37. Second Massacre

The Bunker was no longer a murder scene, it had been two weeks since the first massacre; Cabal Elders were allowed to return. The work to be completed was a summary of voluminous research, and the election of a new Superior Grand Supervisor.

A pro tem Elder spoke from the dais, "Brethren, we have just survived a second trial by fire! The Lord saw what was happening in our little circle. The Devil himself entered the body of one of our own!

A chorus from the assembled rose to a crescendo, "Tell us! Tell us! How many were killed? Who was the murderer? Tell us, Superior Grand Supervisor!"

"Brethren, PLEASE! One moment! *A Brother from the audience spoke.* Have you forgotten how we begin each Meeting?

Show respect to our Superior Grand representative of our Lord! Let us begin.

Lord, hear our prayer...

To **H**old Thy chalice in heart and hand,
To **O**ffer daily prayer for the anointed,
To **P**otentiate our usefulness in Thy service,
To **S**ubmit to Thee forever, Oh Lord!

To Change our worldly thinking and action to har-
monize with Thy will,
    To Offer myself to Thee for salvation of my soul,
    To Teach your Holy Words to all who will listen,
    To Comply with all thy Laws, where ever they lead,
    To Hate not mine enemies, AMEN

"You may be seated, Brothers." The Grand Supervisor left the lectern to stand closer to the assembled
Faithful. "Brothers, there are those in our midst who
would see our precious Lord ridiculed in the courts of
our beloved country. Never in the history of our con-
gregation have we witnessed the work of the devil so
close at hand. The stench of his work could overcome
anyone of you if you were to drop your guard for
even a moment! Questions have been raised about
our work; couched in words that ask 'what are they
really doing,' or 'which country do they represent? And
worse yet, they question our motives as a 'secreted'
organization! My, God! We meet in places such as this
because worldly possessions mean little to us! We
are thrifty so that the word of our Blessed Lord can
continue to bring peace to the tormented, and solace
to weary of mind and body! The Lord has never let us
down! His legions will continue to grow! Threats are
no concern to us as we stand shoulder to shoulder to
meet the foe! This is only a test of our faith! We have,
for years, and will continue to Witness for our Lord, no
matter the consequences! Those assembled in this
room will reap, many fold, the goodness and care the
Father gives his children! Harden not your hearts to

the threats of others. Let His love swell in your being; His love, bringing new life and strength where once there was a question! Lift up your voices as we sing praises to our Lord."

The Faithful began to sing, "Give Praise to Jehovah, his Kingdom Devine, the light that is shining, hi..."

Four masked men flung open the steel door to the assembly room producing a near-deafening sound! The tallest of the four yelled, "Sit down and shut up! The first to move gets a surprise! And, that means you, Mr. Grand What-Ever-The-Hell!"

"I'm sorry I can't oblige you at this moment, you see you have chosen a very poor time to interrupt this peaceful gathering. I'm quite certain your day would improve if you could see your way clear to join..." The report of a handgun caused the beloved Superior Grand Supervisor to slump to the floor in a fetal position.

"I don't think so!" When he was sure he had everyone's attention, he started to make his way down the back, row stopping in front of the first man. "Put your cash and your jewelry into this bag, NOW!" *The man complied, placing a single dollar bill into the bag.* "So, you are the SMART GUY in this room, huh? Well, try this on for size!" He hit the man across the side of his head with the butt of his gun. When the injured man remained standing, the tall man hit him again! "So, Mr. Smart Man, you finally got my message! Gemme your jewelry, NOW!"

Not waiting for the fallen Brother to attempt an answer, the next Cabal Member said, "We don't wear jewelry! We bow to no graven image; no idols! Our Lord forbids it!" The speaker had a smile on his lips as he crumpled to the floor in response to a bullet.

At that moment, the full assembly stood and began singing…to the top of their collective voices, "Give praise to Jehovah, His Kingdom Device, the light that is shin…" Every voice stopped when the first hundred rounds sprayed across the seated men. One of the three remaining men in black, at the front of the room, was laughing as the clip from his Oozy fell empty to the floor. "You take over, Sup. After all, this is really your party, not ours." The FBI Supervisor rose to his feet, "I paid you well. You missed a few back here."

A momentary hush fell over the room. The few remaining began to sing until the last voice was stilled. *Had they been given the opportunity to speak, after the fact, they would have reported that it must have been the same men who were responsible for the first massacre; their threats and manner mimicked each other.*

∾

The FBI Supervisor explained to the responding police that when he entered the assembly room his purpose was to question the attendees about the woman who had been murdered. Then, in a very dramatic voice he preceded to tell how he quickly assessed the situation, spotting the gunmen, and in the attempt to quell the massacre, he shouted, "FBI" and was forced to return fire on each of the four men...killing all of them. *After the assembled were dead! There was no longer a possibility of a witness!* He didn't tell the police he had taken the time to confiscate and temporarily hide the new-found file boxes of Cabal research, spelling-out more possible locations of the missing gold. His greed bolstered his ego...which in turn gave him a sense of incredible power! Power that would allow him to say or do anything he wished, with the prime objective of becoming 'The Most Powerful Man In The World!'

38. Em's Wife Is Missing

"Loved the sleep, loved my breakfast, and more than anything I…LOVE…YOU! How did you get here so soon?"

Janice just flashed a huge smile and grabbed Jac's hand.

Jac and Janice kissed before entering the office. "I'm beginning to really like this. Even when it's out in public."

Janice pulled free, "Glad you do! However, I'm getting a bit tired of sleeping in my apartment ALONE! Janice gave a small punch to Jac's shoulder, "As for this being PUBLIC; Some public! A poorly lit second floor of a nineteen-something year- old building and the only other tenant is taking the day off!"

Jac ignored most of what was said, "So, what! Oh, darn there goes the phone and the lock is stuck. Maybe you can coax it into opening."

"Yes, Sir! Boss!" The door gave way without so much as a whimper. Janice hurried toward the phone. Her usual salutation was followed by an elongated period of silence; then she continued, "No, AJ. We stopped to get a bite then came straight to the office."

A short pause, "No. Em is not with us, he wanted to go home. It seems his wife has been keeping stranger hours than we three have. Do you want to speak to Jac? No? Okay, I'll tell him what you said." Janice turned to Jac, "Agent Croft wants us to bring Em to the FBI office as soon as possible. He said something terrible has happened and we should be with Em when he talks to him."

"My God! What do you think has happened? And, how can it have anything to do with Em?" Jac though for a moment, "I'll bet he's still at Ollie's! Do we have their number?"

Janice was ahead of him, the restaurant phone was ringing, "Hi, my boss and I left you about forty minutes ago, and our friend stayed to finish his Daily Special and read the paper. In fact, all three us had the Special and sat in Booth Ten. Is he still there?" *Pause* "How long ago did he leave?" She cradled the phone, "He's been gone about ten minutes. Shall we drive to his home or wait until we think he's there?"

"I think we should drive now, if AJ wants him as soon as possible it sounds pretty serious to me."

෩

Em was in the open garage sorting through a steamer trunk, "Hey, what are you guys doing here? As for myself, I've been trying to find out what the 'H-E-double-toothpicks' she's been doing? I went to get the bank book so I could cash a check. Do you think it was in its usual location? NO! God only knows where it is hiding! This woman has never, I mean NEVER been careless with anything akin to money! I'm the one who usually does dumb things with money."

Em and Jac looked at each for a split second and began to laugh!

Feeling left out, Janice asked,"Okay, Guys! What the big joke, I want in on the story!"

Em told about the holes drilled in his kitchen wall, the hundred dollar bills and the fire. By the time he finished everyone laughed until they had tears. AJ was not in their 'line of sight' at the time.'

"So, where do you think your wife is today?" Jac wanted to help.

"I don't have the slightest! I guess we have been so busy that we haven't included her yet. And, since we sleep in separate beds I don't even see her when I get home because she gets mad if I disturb her when she is reading." Em paused as though remembering something, "Come to think of it, she hasn't been the same, and she has never fully explained about the man I saw running out of her bedroom that night."

"Enough, Guys. I just remembered why Jac and I are here! We are supposed to take you to AJ's office right now!"

Em continued to sort. "You guys just want me to go to the office so WE can get something accomplished for a change. You'll just have to wait until I find where she hid the check book."

"Janice was telling you the truth. We have to take you to AJ's office NOW! His orders. I think it must be very important! He took the time to call. He usually has a secretary call."

∽

No one acknowledged their presence as they passed the cubicles that made up the FBI offices. AJ was waiting for them. "Come in for a minute." His look told them his news was distressing. "Em, we need to know if you can identify the body of the woman Janice was accused of killing."

Janice and Jac grabbed for Em as he began to sink to the floor.

AJ continued, "I hate like Hell to do this to you, but I thought it would be easier if your mates were with you. Usually a stranger just goes to your home and tell you very little."

No one seemed to notice Janice became several shade whiter when AJ mentioned the Cabal.

A drink of water brought Em to a point where he was able to thank AJ for his consideration. "And, do you know for sure that it's Clarisa? Could it be some-one who looks like her?"

"Unfortunately, no." AJ gave Em's hand an affec-tionate pat. Sorry, but no, a bankbook was found hid-den in her bra. The gunmen had gleaned most of the valuables from the assembled before they were killed."

It was more of a gasp than a whimper. Em seemed to have lost his will to breathe.

Janice had other thoughts on her mind, "AJ, how were the Police notified of the problem?" *She couldn't bring herself to say 'massacre,' but she wanted to know everything! She had a sick feeling her FBI Supervisor had something to do with the event."* Only the FBI Supervisor knew about the Bunker, how did you find out about it?"

Em was clutching for something, anything! "Don't end your sentences with a –"

Everyone helped, ".... a preposition!"

Jac couldn't help himself, "Leave it to our friend to fill it in; In a clutch!" He put his arm over Em's shoulder, "Friend, all of us are going with you and, if in truth it's Clarisa, we will be with you ALL THE WAY! You can count on us, including AJ."

"More than truth be told, Em." The State Agent, turned FBI 'person' had a sobering tone to his voice.

Janice's question brought everyone back to the present. "How *did* you find out about the event?" Jac wasn't sure what it all meant.

"That was the lucky part of this tragedy, Our FBI Supervisor happened to be on his way there to question some of the Cabal followers about the dead woman's murder. When he went into the meeting he was faced with four men dressed in black and guns blazing. He was forced to defend himself. Sadly, by the time he realized what was going down everyone had been killed. He must be a great 'shot,' he was able to get all four gunmen."

Janice was neither surprised nor satisfied. "I just wonder how it was that he was in the perfect place at the perfect time? No one enjoys that kind of pure luck! At least not in my book!"

"Janice, I take an oath, I don't know what you are talking about. It sounds like an 'insinuation' to me. If you know something you consider pertinent to this case you should tell me."

"Sorry, at the moment I don't know whom to trust! Forget what I've just said, let's just help Em." Janice gave him a huge hug. Em clasped her hand, refusing to let go until they reached the Georgia Street Morgue around the corner from FBI offices.

The three friends sat quietly while AJ cut through some of the necessary business attendant to murder. He returned with a small envelope of Clarisa's belongings; a checkbook and a small necklace that looked like an odd-shaped cross. "I guess I have everything. Shall we go?"

Jac nervously adjusted his tie in such a way he was able to finger the like-object hanging under his shirt. He could only wonder the true significance of the 'hopscotch lagger.'

                        ᕤ

It had taken the better part of a week to help Em settle his affairs. He packed out and found an apartment in Jac's building. His home sold within three days and escrow would close in a month. Clarisa's death was a final chapter on an unhappy alliance. He still marveled at the circumstances that brought the three friends together. In fact, the new relationships were respon-sible for quieting the unease he felt with Clarisa. He hadn't realized how her overbearing manner had shaped his former, buffoon like behavior.

Jac was the one who encouraged Em to find respect for himself. Em now had purpose. He knew Jac was proud of his efforts...he had told him so on numerous occasions.

The Mighty Three agreed it felt great to be back in their office.

"Janice, why don't you and Em join me for the conference I'm to have with AJ. I promised to meet with him as soon as we had 'office business' set-up and Em's affairs in order."

"Do you think he will tell us about the game Brooks' was playing? If, in fact it was only a game."

"I don't know. I'm as interested to know as you are! Boy, what a mess!"

"At least, it's not our mess!"

∾

39. Eights Krister

One would have to agree, the FBI office was a little brighter and more appropriately furnished than the last time the three visited.

"Great to see the three of you! Enjoy yourselves, have a seat. Don't the new chairs feel great? Little by little, I plan to see the that the office looks more professional." AJ pushed a couple of card tables in front of his guests.

Jac flashed a puzzled look towards Janice, "Have you been made Chief or something, AJ?"

"More like 'or something.' I want to bring the three of you up to speed on something VERY important. A National Security issue, and you, my friend are right in the cross-hairs." Agent Croft was looking directly at Jac.

"Thanks for nothing, AJ, You just made the hairs stand-up on the back of my neck. What's this all about?"

"Quite simply, the twelve gold railroad spikes stolen from a Government museum."

Jac interrupted, "I thought, before when you mentioned this, you said they were taken from a private collection. Governor Stanford's, to be exact. How did the Government get involved?"

"Politics, my friend. Simply stated, the Government learned about thirteen spikes being struck, and not just the one used at Promontory Point. Can you even begin to imagine the political power attendant to twelve golden spikes said to be struck in the image of Christ's twelve apostles? We mistakenly thought the cult was responsible. That's why we called it Operation Hopscotch. A bidding war has continued to heat up since the theft was discovered. At last word, the Vatican has now offered two billion American dollars. Our Government has refused to talk about payment …to ANYONE! And, somebody said the heirs are ready to do anything to retrieve them from our Government. The FBI has been commissioned to find the spikes."

Jac stood up and faced AJ full-faced, "How in the name of all that's Holy am I involved?"

"It's really your family more than you. It seems your birthplace has being identified as a possible location of the stolen spikes. From what I understand, Warsaw was quite the hub of some very important Governmental decisions from the early 1880s. Some have boasted that Warsaw's central location was considered for the prime location for the Nation's Capitol. My take on its history and the City's involvement in our mystery was its prominence as a railroad hub serving several of the nation's first major railroads… including the Gold-Spike Railroad. I understand the City is very near the Mississippi River. I guess early

investors could see the potential for developing manu-
facturing plants that could disperse goods by way of
the river. So, think of it, how easy would it be to trace
the 'tracks' of earlier railroad investors, say, 1869 for
example, to Warsaw, Illinois as a convenient place
to hide the spikes. Better yet! Think! Could there be
a better or easier location to hide the spikes than the
Depot Hotel? According to our investigation."

Janice took Jac's hand, "What's wrong? You look
terrible! Are you Okay? Say something!"

Jac's vacant stare, coupled with a barely audible
response, was enough for AJ to suggest they break
for some supper. The Pantry was the closer of two
available restaurants. When the steaks and garlic
bread were consumed, Jac spoke, "I believe I have a
clearer understanding of my part in this preposterous
situation! First off! I don't appreciate having my family
involved! Secondly! Janice, who the hell is your FBI
Supervisor and why did he send us to Illinois without
telling AJ?"

AJ directed his question to Janice, "Jac just took
the words out of my mouth! What is the answer, if in
fact you know *anything* about all of this?"

Janice was about to cry, "I've told Jac and Em
everything I know about the Supervisor and the trip!"
She began to sob, "I di..didn't want to go! I di..didn't
wa..wan..want to carr..y my piece! He tried to se..sex..
sexually att..attack me several times! Oh, Jac! You
HAVE to believe me! I only know about the religion, I
don't know any..."

Agent Croft broke-in, "WHAT religion?"

Em spoke his first words in a very long time, "This isn't the place for questions, let's get out of here! I don't much care to see Janice hurt." Em glared at both AJ and Jac.

"I agree with you, Em. Let's get back to my office and see if we can make some sense out of *any* of this!"

෴

The unfinished, FBI lunch room became a dual-purpose lounge for comfortable, *private* seating and snacking room…thanks to the 'do not disturb' sign AJ hung on the outside doorknob.

Jac and AJ were still apologizing when a telephone rang. "Yes, I heard what you said. Yes, I appreciate the heads up! Yes, I do want to speak with you before you write your report. No! I want you to come to the office now! No! Not later! Now." A thinner 'voice' added, I have someone here who would very much like to review your information. By the way, I'm in the lunchroom."

The three looked at each other.

"Please excuse me as I make a call." AJ sat more erect and his voice powerful! "Get Washington for me. Tell them the pigeon is returning to his roost. I would like to have you as my backup if needed. *Pause* "No."*Pause* "True."*Long pause* "You can never tell what a terrorist and traitor will do. I'm counting on your team. Yes. Thanks."

AJ turned to the little group, "Well, that's taken care of for the time being."

"Do you mind telling the three of us what that was all about?"

"Sure, Jac. The three of you have been instrumental, albeit by blind luck, in bringing one of the most cunning enemies of the Country to his knees!

Most of the credit goes to you, Janice. Without you passion for justice and your love of Country we could NEVER have challenged his ego in the same, successful way as you did. Your Country owes you. As for the two of you, well, what can I say?"

"You could say, I'll take you home now." Em was smiling, a broad friendly smile.

AJ chuckled, "Ever the optimist! I don't blame you, Em. Unfortunately, You have just begun your work with this office. I know you will be please when you hear what we have planned for the three of you."Agent Croft was interrupted by a knock at the door.

"Please, come in, Supervisor Krister."

Jac couldn't shake an *instinctive* foreboding, *"Where have I heard that name before? No matter, I'll probably remember in the middle of the night. I just can't shake it! Why do I know that name?"*

The three friends stood frozen to the spot. No one was aware that Janice's knees were quivering. Only the visitor and Agent Croft saw Janice's eyes react to the shock of being face to face with her Supervisor, and her fear of possible retaliation for giving up information about the Cabal.

AJ stood and extended his hand, "Supervisor Krister, I believe you know everyone."

The Supervisor was triumphant! He even stood a bit taller than his usual squat stature. *I love the 'hero' role!* "Yes, I do, Croft." Turning to better see Janice, he continued," Good to see all of you again. And, you, Young Lady, I should scold you! You were supposed to check-in with me after your release from the San Pedro jail. No matter, I forgive you this time." *His lecherous smile caused Em to throw away his sandwich and leave the room…without a bye or leave.* "Something I said?" Still riding high from his recent triumph, the Supervisor flashed a smile that said it all! *'I, Supervisor Krister, am – IN CONTROL!'*

"Have a seat, Krister! I would like a summary of what happened at the Bunker?"

The Supervisor flashed another Napoleonic smile, "Croft, haven't you forgotten something? I DON'T report in front of civilians!"

Agent Croft continued in carefully, measured syllables, "Krister! You are the ONLY civilian in this room!" He retrieved a large manila envelope from his desk drawer, "Give me you badge, your gun, and bank checks!"

Krister looked like an inflatable that had just been pierced. "You don't have the right to do this!" It was more of a whimper than a statement.

"On the contrary, I have every right to do whatever I believe to be right. I have neglected to tell all of you that I am now, the new Director of the FBI"

Audible sounds of shock and surprise filled the little lunchroom. Jac was the first to stand, with hand extended he shook the Director's hand, "They made the perfect choice, AJ!"

"Thanks, Jac. I appreciate the kind words. I expect to count on you and your cohorts for support in finding the gold spikes."

A gasp and stifled scream from Krister's direction, "No! You can't! You FOOLS! You have NO right! They belong to me!"

"Glad you mentioned the subject of 'ownership.' We are assigning the new recruits to summarize the research you commissioned your Cabal followers to collect for you!"

A wide-eyed Krister asked, "How the HELL do you know about that? I was so careful!"

"Krister, have you forgotten everything you ever knew about detection? We have been investigating you since Agent Marrs refused to take some of the assignments that included you as principal Agent. You have been under full surveillance, including but not limited to, wire-tap and cameras at EVERY location you frequented." Croft stopped when he heard Krister's audible "NO!"

Jac threw-up both arms and screamed, "I KNOW WHO HE IS! I KNOW WHO HE IS! Or. Least who he is related to! I remember the name!"

Director Croft broke-in, "Jac, what wrong? What are you talking about? Take it easy!"

"I Can't help it, AJ! I know who he is! And, I think I know where the spikes are!"

"Who do you think he is and where do you think the spikes are? My God, are you certain? I Just can't believe this! Tell me who is he?"

Former Agent Krister sat crying. He just kept repeating that the spikes belonged to him.

Jac cleared his throat, "My God, I just can't believe this. I'm trying to remember what my dad used to say about old, "Eights Krister." I recall he said the man was a well known and a well respected surveyor responsible for finding the best lands for the railroads. My dad loved to prophesize about what would be happening, in my time. He talked about a network of rails that that would soon cross the country like a spider's web. I guess he wasn't a complete fool! I rode one of those trains to get here." Jac stopped his reverie and straightened a bit, as if to recall something to mind. "I figure the Supervisor must be his grandson or some relative. I'm glad old Krister isn't alive to witness a relative become as infamous as old Doc Mudd!"

"Jac, I don't think you have to worry about the Krister Family name...this man was just a want-to be relative!"

The three on-lookers remained wordless as the exchange of information continued between Croft and Jac.

"You said you think you know where the spikes are located."

"Yes! The way my dad told it was, old Eights spent a lot of time in Warsaw, in fact he was the one to survey land for the Golden spike Railroad which later to became the Detroit, Indiana and something. I just don't remember much about that part of the story. But, at about the same time the courthouse and the Depot Hotel were being built. According to dad, the interesting information was the trouble they had trying to 'balance' the two-ton bell in the clock tower of the Court House. Dad said there was a real hue and cry about the fact that the bell was *in balance* when it was delivered... contending something had to have happened to it to cause the disequilibrium." Jac became more animated, "So? What do you think?"

Krister began screaming, "Stop it! Stop it! God DAMN it! His name wasn't Eights Krister! It was Amos Thompson Shaw Krister!

Just because he used the three initials in his name the local jackasses called him 'Eights' instead of A period, T period, S period, Krister!"

No one was interested in Krister's problem. Croft just wanted to learn more. "Jac, I don't have a clue what you're talking about. Are you saying the spikes have something to do with the bell's problem?"

"Well, think about it, AJ. What if you wanted to hide heavy, spike-sized hunks of gold, what would you look for? Wouldn't you want to find something so heavy no one would be likely to investigate, because of its location and heft?"

Croft's face brightened, "By God, you could be right!" He turned to catch Em and Janice's attention. "Are the two of you up to a second trip to Illinois?

Supervisor Krister began screaming. This time, Director Croft opened the door and asked his 'back-up' to remove the traitor.

∽

40. Loose Ends

The little office on Fifth Street, most likely had never seen this much celebration. Champagne glasses were filled to the brim for each of the several 'toasts' given. Each of the four friends took turns recognizing the fetes of the others…especially Jac's prowess in solving the location of the missing spikes! The room was filled with excited, half-finished discussions about the events of the last couple of weeks. Questions were being thrown, one to another, hoping to get clarification on most of the bizarre events.

"How long did the FBI know Krister was 'double-dealing?'"

"What did 'Hopscotch' mean?"

"Why did Cabal members wear the 'lagger-thing?'" "Was Jac's dad really involved?" "How about the murders…were they connected to the Cabal of The Devine?"

More importantly, how was it that the three, office friends became acquainted, and who was instrumental in putting Jac in the position to 'save the day' for Janice, Em, the FBI, Cabal Faithful, as well as himself?"

Newly appointed FBI Director Croft opened a large notebook. "I think the easiest way to bring you folks up to speed is to read part of the text written in Agent Riddle's report. You may find some of this grammatically lacking...and please forgive his over-use of paraphrasing:

A Compilation of Cabal Investigation [A two week period]
It will be much easier to lay-out the events if I work backwards:

The little town of Warsaw, Illinois according to National and International News:
"....enjoyed a fast five minutes of fame as workers freed the golden spikes from the under-side of the Court House Bell. The US Government was overjoyed to receive them!" The Catholics Church and The Masons will no doubt litigate for years to come, each holding out for a win.

Nicus (nickname)Cartwright: father of Jac Cartwright has vowed to delete his son from his will. He referred to his son as an ingrate! Giving information that left his own father out of the contest for the gold spikes! *He, the father, who had, spent the last ten* years 'replicating' (with his own verbiage) the pages that he would one day be used *to 'free the spikes'* *from their hiding place!"*

Pages that even fooled the Supervisor! NOW... *it was... ALL OVER! "Nothing left for him! Seeing as how it was HE, Dad, who was responsible for concocting, with quill pen, much of the 'revelations' directed toward expository evidence of a possible "Chosen One," (Jacques Braden Cartwright)." And, location of the golden spikes!*

Mr. Cartwright was LIVID during most of our inter-rogations! Granted, the fraud would have been a huge coup for the old man! He said he, could have man-aged his son to new heights of fame…and money!

I don't think he knew his son was only interested in a law practice.

I'll bet he never discussed anything with his son. From what I gathered, he was too busy maintaining a bombastic, and controlling manner throughout the few years he had with his son.

He said, he himself would have been more suc-cessful than Johnny Sunday who went from town to town spreading 'salvation.' And here, after all those years he toiled on the 'research.' And all the material he was "intelligent" enough to create…his work is for naught! He said at the time he was glad the family ignored his 'ramblings' at the dinner table. "Little did they know, the rambling were rehearsal" for the next pages of "local history" he would be creating in the morning! He laughed when he told me how he cov-ered his absences from home by telling the family he was still trying to square a sphere. You have to give the man credit for thinking up the scheme. Unfortu-nately, he soundsa bit off center.

259

As for Mr. Krister, he isn't now, or ever has been related to the famous Krister. I learned he adopted the name and family history to serve as evidence of his illustrious lineage.

Respectfully Submitted by,
Riddle, Agent FBI

Director Croft, replaced the report, "I think that's the sum and substance of Riddle's information. The rest of your questions will have to wait until we are ready to close this case." Croft closed his file and refilled his drink.

The office celebration waned a bit, but only to a point where Croft nearly waxed poetic as he summarized his take on the events of the last month.

"To begin with, we are certain the Cabal of the Devine is no more than a conglomerate mix of International Bible Students, some of whom still follow Pastor Russ's teachings from the early twenties; others, follow the words of the Judge who figured out that if they would give up their pride about…not being a religion, they could own property…tax free; and collectively they have accomplished, single-handedly, the salvation of a derelict Warsaw printing company; thought to be doomed by neglect and decay. But the Cabal Faithful have turned everything around! They have taken a cavernous basement filled with books, some new, some old…with rolls and reams of unused paper and turned the resources into manna from heaven. They will no longer have to drag those heavy, phonographs from door to door; Telling about possible salvation. Now they will have brightly colored books and leaflets to publish. I've heard they plan to change the name to The Golden Word Publishing Society. Imagine, a free workforce, free paper, free ink and a wealth of research..too old for copyright! What a gift from God! God Bless them all! If they don't wake up, someone else will find them ripe for the picking! Their local membership has really been thinned! Thanks to, Krister! Not to worry, they seem determined to continue their work. We consider them a "No Harm, No Foul" segment of society. I wish them well."

Croft took a swallow of his drink, "As for the two massacres, and Em's wife, anyone who knew too much had to be killed! Em's wife knew too much! She was one very smart lady! Just not smart enough to see through Krister's cunning scheme. I think she really believed she was helping our Country."

"On the other hand, our worthy FBI Supervisor, aka Grand Supervisor of the Cabal of the Devine gave us a real run for our money. You have to give the Devil his dues, the man had talent for 'achievement,' even more then he was aware of, had he been 'more aware' he would have probably ended up as Director of the FBI!"

The room suddenly filled with an assortment of spontaneous laughter.

"Okay, you three can laugh all you want, but that man almost did just that! He had accumulated an enviable list of supporters. It could have happened!"

Croft continued, "Anyway, about the 'hopscotch' thing. As much as we were able to learn, the necklace was the symbol of a combination of tenets the Cabal held dear. The cross-like design was fashioned, including numbered squares, like the child's game of hopscotch. The First square was 'Baptism,' the Second, 'denouncing worldly-goods,' Third, 'study to show thy self approved,' Fourth and Fifth, the two periods of 'Daily Devotion' and 'Prayer,' the Sixth, was 'glean the field for Believers,' and the Seventh, 'suffer the trials and tribulation of Satan and inherit the earth!' Unfortunately, a single mis-step along the way held the penalty of "starting from the beginning and receiving dispensation" from a Cabal Supervisor when deemed appropriate. Oh, I almost forgot, there was some question about the material the necklace was made of; interesting, but probably unimportant. They never thought of it as jewelry, only a guide from God." Croft cleaned his glasses, "Theirs was not an easy game to play!"

Croft turned to face Jac, "I wanted you to know the Brooks' case is over and done with! The poor man was being used by some locals who needed a place to test the Jap transistors and found Brooks to be the perfect Patsy! He would do anything for more money; even when he thought he was cheating our government. Well, they had the last laugh because it's believed they were able to sell Disney on buying their product which should mean millions for Disney!

Croft pulled a page from his valise, "As for your dad; I'm sure you realize your father is a very, very intelligent man, not to smart maybe, but very intelligent.

It's too bad his greed overcame his need to achieve. The two of you could have had a great life! It seems to me your mom is going to be just fine. I guess I didn't tell you what our infamous Supervisor did; in fact, with your father's permission. They had mom on drugs so that she would pose no threat to the pact the two had entered into on behalf of getting 'filthy rich'... according to your Dad's statement. Krister lied about being willing to share the gold. I would prefer not to know, how your father will react when he learns he truth."

Jac, mumbled softly, "My God! I could have lost my mom as well as loosing dad. Him...I don't mind so much...but mom...I guess, like they say. every boy needs his mom."

"So where do I fit in the picture?" Janice's eyes glistened.

"Me, too?" Hardly more than a plaintive sound from, Em.

"Croft, wouldn't you think that these two would know how deeply set they are in my life?"

"Perhaps you need to tell them in 'words' for a change. I get the impression you want everyone to read your mind Jac. I don't think that works too well." Turning to face the three of them, Croft spoke. "We will still need your help from time to time. The three of you work so well together, and since each of you contributed to the FBI's success in this matter, I would like to know if you can help with a new case... we're calling it 'Operation: Dodge Ball'" This would be right up your alley, Em! Good investigators are at a premium. And I know you love the Farmer's Market! Why don't you take Jac for a visit. Plan to have lunch on us…I'll join you if time allows." *Long pause* "So, what do you folks say?"

Em was excited, "Count me in!"

"Suits me, too… if Janice still wants to be with me. I made a promise to her and I would like to keep it!"

Janice flashed a wide smile, "Of course. After all, a promise is a …PROMISE!"

Jac ignored her insinuation, "I'm also anxious to catch up on things in the office. I'm happy to assist if and only if I can manage both my law practice and the FBI. I was thinking that it might be workable if Janice and I take care of most of the office responsibilities and you utilize Em's expertise when I don't need him."

"Sounds workable, Jac!" Croft shook everyone's hand, gathered his valise and took a last pull on his drink. "See, You!"

Jac sat back in his chair, "Before I do anything else, I'm going to make a quick trip home to make sure my mom and sis are okay. At no time, did I imagine my family was under full FBI surveillance. Under the circumstances, Janice, I would like very much if you would accompany me? We will only be gone two days. And, Croft did say we should go. What do you say?"

"Hey, Guys! Croft included me! Croft said I could go!"

"Just wanted to know if you were listening."

THE END

∽

Epilogue

Jac opened a leather bound, letter-sized Daily Journal; a gift from Doc Harks. Jac was ashamed to admit that in the five years since he last met with Doc, it had remained at the bottom of his oldest suitcase, and never touched... or thought of as important. He lifted his pen to write:

I can't help the gnawing discomfort I feel whenever I think of intimacy with Janice. It must be my lack of whatever it takes to trust people. Do I really love her, or am I playing a losing game? Truth is I'm not experienced.

Jac ran his fingers over the scar on each breast and relived the night a young boy became a man,' bloodied, bent, and terrified! He continued writing. *Who knew a Dean and a couple kiss-ass students could not be trusted! Jac allowed a grunt and chuckle to replace what should have been a 'full-out' laugh when he thought of his father.*

My dad! What an imagination! He could have spit tacks the night he found out about the hazing! Man! What a mind! Who else could have seen my scars as a means to get money? Blows my mind! He must have mentally recorded every word spoken in the home. I recall some of the things that upset him the most. Yes! The "twosomes," he called them, that would show up about the time he was listening to a favorite radio program; banging on the door and wanting to know if dad cared about his salvation! If they were fleet of foot they removed themselves before he kicked their phonograph halfway down the hill.

God, I loved those confrontations! But, the old man's brain must have been plotting, even then, to get the best of someone... anyone! He hated the cult so much he probably went to the library, looked them up and decided to see if he could get anyone to take the bait. When he learned about the spikes it didn't take much time for him, to put two and two, plus a par-lay with the information he knew about early Warsaw history... to hatch his clever plan. What a Guy! You have to give him some credit. He aged the paper and wrote in perfect script. If he hadn't boasted of his skills it may have taken much longer to understand the intricacies of his plan. I almost feel a sense of pride. Almost. Not quite. The old Bastard! Why couldn't he have used some of his cunning and pseudo logic to do something of value! Who knows... who cares?

Fortunately, there is Operation Dodge Ball to look forward to. I'm beginning to wonder if I'm afraid to get that first Case into court. God, I hope not! The money for Operation: Hopscotch was mighty sweet! Guess I'll get Janice a ring, when I win my that Case! Oh, yes! I am relieved learn Mom and Sis are fine; at least, mom will be fine in a week or so. Guess freedom from drugs, and Dad's absence for a few weeks will work wonders for both her and Sis! The worst of the nightmare is over. Can't wait to see mom and sis tomorrow!

Goodnight, Self

The leather bound journal was replaced at the bottom of the old suitcase.

Author's Biography

An Illinois woman who fell in love with California and Arizona; the warmer climes. Widowed, mother of two, at age 60 I vowed to pursue a formal education. Call this my third career...stay at home mom, and dedicated community volunteer. Fifty-three, continuous years for the American and International Red Cross and now author. I worked seventy to eighty hours a week to gain "experience hours," and went to school full time. Fourteen years later I was enjoying a licensed, professional career serving the needs of families in trouble; and, even better I was teaching college and university students.

This "my first book" was written for the many women and men, who like I, suffer from the "Imposter Syndrome." You are certain that you could NEVER do, some-something your heart of hearts, wishes you could do! Now, for myself, when that little, niggling feeling allows a "doubt" to creep into my zone, I can review my evidence of success! So, WOMEN and MEN, start your "Evidence" TODAY! Do anything that would make you, even more proud, of your Actions and achievements! And, to anyone who said you couldn't do anything right...TOO BAD!

If I can...YOU CAN! Best of Everything to your successes! Let me know how you are doing talkdoc@cox.net

www.ingramcontent.com/pod-product-compliance
Lightning Source LLC
Chambersburg PA
CBHW031300170626
46807CB00001B/239